A New Leash on Life

A New Leash on Life

Book 9

Dragonfly Cove Dog Park Series

Patricia Sands

A NEW LEASH ON LIFE
A novel
by Patricia Sands

A NEW LEASH ON LIFE is a work of fiction. Names, characters, places and incidents either are products of the author's imagination or are used fictitiously. Any resemblance to actual events, locales, entities, or persons, living or dead, is entirely coincidental.

A NEW LEASH ON LIFE Copyright © 2025 by Patricia Sands.

All rights reserved. No part of this book may be reproduced or transmitted in any form or by any means, electronic or mechanical including photocopying, recording, or by any information storage and retrieval system without the written permission of the author, except for the use of brief quotations in a book review. No AI Training: without in any way limiting the author's and publisher's exclusive rights under copyright, any use of this publication to "train" generative artificial intelligence (AI) technologies to generate net is expressly prohibited. The author reserves all rights to license uses of this work for generative AI training and development of machine learning language models. For permissions contact the author directly via electronic mail: psandsstories@gmail.com

ISBN 978-1-0691281-0-2

FIRST EDITION Cover by Elizabeth Mackey Graphic Design

Printed in the United States of America

This story is dedicated to Annie McDonnell who loves dogs almost as much as she loves books.

Also by Patricia Sands

Lost at Sea (Book 8 in the Sail Away Series)

The Secrets We Hide

The Bridge Club

The Promise of Provence (Love in Provence Book 1)

Promises to Keep (Love in Provence Book 2)

I Promise You This (Love in Provence Book 3)

Drawing Lessons

The First Noël at the Villa des Violettes (Villa des Violettes Book 1)

A Season of Surprises at the Villa des Violettes (Villa des Violettes Book 2)

Lavender, Loss & Love at the Villa des Violettes (Villa des Violettes Book 3)

Deck the Halls at the Villa des Violettes (Villa des Violettes Book 4)

Chapter One

The business of aging was not quite as Libby and Don Moore had imagined it would be. They had envisioned an idyllic retirement in their lifelong home of Dragonfly Cove, just as their parents had enjoyed.

Everything had gone well until three years ago when the roof fell in, so to speak. This time it had not been a Florida hurricane doing the damage.

It had been a diagnosis delivered by their good friend and family physician, Doctor Alfredo Lopez.

"Don, I'm sorry to say that our tests show you have the beginning stages of dementia. I'm sorry, Don ... and Libby,"

His words hung in the air before he continued.

"I know this is a shock."

He had delivered the diagnosis gently, his voice soft and low, as Libby clutched Don's hand. A tidal wave of emotions rushed through her, but all Libby could think of was how she could help Don. He did not deserve this.

In the early days after the distressing revelation, Don had tried to talk to Libby about how her life should continue on. That had been difficult and painful for both of them. He had been so courageous and realistic.

※ ※
※ ※

The dementia progressed quickly in the three years that followed.

Only sixty-three when it was discovered Don was not simply being forgetful, now his condition left him dependent on daily care and increasingly unaware of his surroundings. Libby and their ten-year-old rescue cats, siblings Max and Mimi, were the only parts of his life he acknowledged in his last few months at home. Although he then called Libby and both the cats, Louie.

The only relief Libby could see in the months before he moved to full-time care, was how calming the cats were for Don and how the fluffy felines seemed to know this was their role. There were few times during the day and night that one or both of them was not curled up on his lap or snuggled beside him in bed.

The two silvery grey, long-haired tabby cats came from a litter of newborns discovered in a dumpster. These two immediately found a loving home with Libby and Don.

Each had a distinctive personality and, at ten years, continued to be rambunctious. Mimi loved her toys and Max was the hunter, proudly depositing his catches of mice, moles and the occasional baby iguana at the back door. Evening zoomies were guaranteed by both of them as they raced around the house, taking turns chasing each other.

As time went on, Don simply gazed into space and reacted to nothing but the cats. Libby felt her darling husband was floating in a pool of lost memories. She understood when dementia was described as death before dying and it broke her heart to watch it play out.

Their son, Matthew, his wife Amy, and the grandchildren, Jack, 15, and Kate, 13, had been caring and attentive as Don's illness progressed. But in time, Don had no response to them either. It was sad and painful for everyone.

Libby knew they felt Don's absence. Even the cats did.

Shortly after they finalized all the details of Don's move to full-time care, Matthew was advised he and his family soon were being sent off by his company to Australia for a three-month assignment.

"All of a sudden I am going to be quite alone. It's amazing how quickly our lives can change." Libby had exclaimed to Matt and Amy. They promised her they would be in constant touch and the time would fly by.

Jack and Kate excitedly assured their beloved Grandma that they were already looking forward to returning home. "We've got a puppy to pick up the week after we get back!"

Libby worried they were taking on too much by having an 8-week old yellow Labrador retriever puppy on their hands while they resettled back in Dragonfly Cove.

She mentioned to friends more than once, "Better them than me! Imagine all the work that a pup involves! But they say they know what they are doing and that they will all pitch in, so I'm certain they will."

There were times a dark cloud of loss hovered over her as her life changed.

She accepted that living alone would be the next chapter in her life. It wasn't the being alone part but rather the absence of the man she had loved so completely for so long. Libby had many friends and an active social life that revolved around hiking and tennis, even while she still worked.

Don had also been a part of those activities. Carrying on with them kept continuity in her life. But his absence was glaring to her.

They had been so young when they first found each other. He, the quietly handsome football player who dreamed of coaching kids. She, the sporty but reserved girl who was never without a book.

In their early college days, they met each other in the university library, hiding away from partying friends and trying to focus on studies. They joked about it often as Libby went on to become a librarian and Don an athletic director. It was meant to be ... their union and her devotion to books. She was one of those women who always felt grateful as her life unfolded.

They had imagined they would have more than one child, but it was not to be. As time went by, Libby and Don cherished their son Matthew and the family he grew up to bless them with.

Through the years, friends teased Don and Libby about the happy activity-filled life they built around careers they loved. They appreciated all the positives of life and were quick to express these feelings.

Life was good, until it wasn't.

When dementia began to steal Don away, Libby felt she had been blindsided. This was not how it was meant to be.

Libby could not stop thinking about how quickly life can change when least expected, with Don now living in Serenity Palms. It would have been wrong to say he was contented since he did not appear to feel anything. He was

A New Leash on Life

not agitated and seemed to simply exist. At least, that was how the medical staff described it to her. They suggested to Libby she should be thankful for that as some residents were troubled and agitated.

Still, it preyed on her mind, particularly in the long lonely evenings. She missed his steady approach to life, his ready laugh, his gentle touch.

The decision to move him to Serenity Palms had not been easy but Libby knew it was the right one. He was safe and well looked after and just a few minutes' drive from their home.

The assisted-living center was brand new and located in the midst of a sprawling oasis with an exceptional variety of stunning palm trees and broad expanses of lawn and flowerbeds.

Everything was designed to give the residents and visitors feelings of tranquility and calm. Gardens overflowed with colorful flowering vegetation including plumbago, lantana, plumeria, ixora, firebush, hibiscus and massive bougainvillea, all dutifully attended by delicate butterflies and busy bees.

Ornamental fountains dotted the vast property. The splashing and bubbling of cascading water brought a sense of cooling to those passing by in the hot, humid weather of Dragonfly Cove.

The gardeners went about their work cheerfully in even the hottest weather. The property was immaculate.

All of the staff in the residence that Libby had met during these past months were warm and knowledgeable. Kindness lived there.

While Libby had struggled with her emotions about Don leaving their home, the doctors and her family supported the decision all the way. Matthew and Amy helped make the move as trouble-free as possible before they left for Australia.

In quiet moments now, when the reality of getting old consumed her thoughts, she felt the worst part of it was dealing with loss. There was loss in your children growing up and leaving the nest, loss of your parents and extended family as time and illness claimed them, loss of friends as they passed and now the loss of her life partner, as well as her satisfying career. It was a time of profound change.

Grateful for her relatively good health, she could deal with the occasional aches and pains from tennis and hiking. With the help of over the counter meds and nothing more, she was determined to meet the physical challenges of aging in the best way possible. So far, she felt she had been lucky and blessed with good genes. Her parents had both lived to ninety years and passed peacefully in their own home.

Wrinkles and grey hair didn't bother her in the least. In fact, she liked her silvery hair and was happy not to spend ridiculous amounts of money on the color and highlights she had kept up for so many years. COVID had changed that.

She read somewhere that wrinkles gave a face warmth and charisma and when she told Don this, years before, he had kissed her and said they showed the kindness by which she lived her life. She had liked that. Goodness knows she was not a saint she thought, but she tried hard to live her best life.

On the wall in her kitchen was a plaque that read "Getting old is not for sissies". She nodded to it every day.

When she turned fifty she promised herself, and Don, she would make every effort to appreciate waking up each morning. In fact, they made a pact they would both keep the mantra that 'every day is a gift'.

Don adopted that as his favorite toast and, until he

A New Leash on Life

began to exhibit signs of his condition, it always made them smile. In Matthew's wedding speech, he had referred to this and vowed he and Amy would try to follow that mantra too.

Libby knew Don had not understood what she was saying when she talked to him about it in recent years. She also knew, if he could have, he still would have agreed wholeheartedly. He was that kind of man ... the glass was always half full ... and she had learned a lot from him in their years together.

One of the best parts of their lives had been the surprising joy of becoming grandparents. They adored Jack and Kate and agreed wholeheartedly with the saying that "you love your children, but you are in love with your grandchildren".

They had been thankful that Matthew and Amy lived close by and welcomed their involvement. The family unit became even closer and filled with love and laughter with the arrival of the two grandchildren so many years ago.

Don always reminded them both that they had to be getting older to have the gift of grandchildren. "You see," he teased, "there are benefits to aging! This and seniors' day at the drugstore."

Chapter Two

In February, after Libby's end of the year retirement from her librarian position in the Dragonfly Cove elementary school, she and her best friend, Marge Bailey, took a trip to Hawaii. Planning and then going on the holiday had been bittersweet.

Libby's cats were settled at Happy Tails Boarding, where she knew they would be pampered and loved.

Marge's handsome and chatty African grey parrot, Einstein, went to stay with her next-door neighbour, who loved the bird and often took care of it.

As they sat on the plane carrying them across the Pacific, Libby confessed that she couldn't relax about the trip until she knew Max and Mimi were happily settled. "Does it sound crazy that I wasn't worried about Don? I knew he would be well looked after. But those cats were another story. It's been a while since I left them."

Marge chuckled and patted Libby's hand. "Don't feel guilty about not worrying how Don would be. You know he is in the best place possible."

Libby gave her a grateful smile. "When I first called to

book the cats a spot, Happy Tails Boarding was full and there was a waiting list. I wouldn't have wanted to leave the cats anywhere else. We got lucky with a cancellation."

Marge looked at her knowingly. "I know what you mean. You are well aware that if Einstein is not happy, I'm not going to enjoy my trip. That bird rules my life. Our pets are almost as much a worry as our kids."

The flight attendant appeared with a tray of flower bedecked tall glasses. "May I interest you ladies in a Blue Hawaiian? It contains rum, cream of coconut, pineapple juice, and curaçao liqueur to create its signature blue color, and is absolutely delicious."

"Why not?" They both answered and then toasted to a great vacation.

"Yum!" Marge murmured. "With the pineapple and coconut flavors, it really tastes like Hawaii!"

Libby was silent for a moment as she enjoyed the cool, refreshing liquid sliding down her throat. "Mmmm! Like a day at the beach."

The drink had just enough alcohol in it to relax Libby and before long she blurted, "Oh Marge, I'm finding this new life of mine to be so much more challenging than I expected. Without Don beside me there's a deep hole in my life and now with retirement ..." her voice trailed off.

Marge nodded. Her voice was sympathetic. "I hear you. It's awful to be without your beloved husband and a job you loved to go to every day. But here's some advice that helped me. Don't think of the word 'retirement'. Instead say rewirement! I read that word somewhere and decided to make it my own. I love that! You can involve yourself in all sorts of changes in your life. It just takes time to adjust. To rewire."

Libby thought quietly for a moment. She savored the last drops of her drink and mulled over Marge's words before she said, "Hey! That's a good one! I like that word too. Okay, I'm going to attempt to become rewired starting now."

She put her head back and let her thoughts flow to positive places. It would take effort, but she was determined she would rewire. She told herself that from now on she was going to focus on the changes she could make to her life in this new chapter on her own.

"I'm going to look into doing more volunteer work and I'm going to donate all of Don's woodworking tools and unfinished projects. It's time I re-organized."

"I think another Blue Hawaiian might be just what we need," Marge said, as she pressed the button for the attendant.

Soon after that second cocktail, they were both fast asleep on the long flight.

The first night on Kauai they relaxed on the spacious terrace of their condo and gazed over a quiet moonlit beach, sipping deliciously fruity mai tai cocktails. They had decided to forego the nightly luau until the next evening.

A gentle breeze rustled through the palm trees carrying with it the sound of harmonious voices, accompanied by the soothing strumming of ukuleles and the rhythmic beating of drums. The strains of melodious tunes of traditional Hawaiian music filled the air.

As the sun dipped low on the horizon, the sky blazed in stunning reds, pinks and gold before delicate shades of blue and purple softened the fiery performance. A shimmering glow spread across the tranquil water before the velvety sky filled with twinkling stars.

"I could get used to this," they commented to each other, grinning.

But in spite of her smile, Don was on Libby's mind. She had never travelled without him before and had no choice but to accept this new reality.

Marge had been divorced for fifteen years and, after a period of grieving and adjusting, she was perfectly content to be on her own. She was sympathetic to Libby's feelings and offered support at all times, but she had found happiness in her independent life.

The stunning natural beauty of the island and the easy approach to life there offered the perfect combination for relaxation. Days passed quickly with long walks on the golden sand of different beaches. Swimming and snorkeling in the calm, crystal clear water were daily pursuits. The women were even convinced to join in the hula lessons around the pool that provided much laughter for all involved.

Treating themselves to a rejuvenating spa day before they left, Marge said, "I could be convinced to live here if it were not for my grandchildren. Now I'm going to enjoy this massage and indulge in the fantasy."

Libby had no trouble agreeing with her, particularly as she breathed in the tropical scented lotions of coconut, pineapple and mango. Stunning plumeria and pikake leis hung everywhere, their fragrances perfuming the air. Paradise through aromatherapy she thought to herself as she inhaled deeply.

Always though, thoughts of Don were never far from her mind. She made a point of not going on about it, but it was difficult.

There were times she was able to give herself permission to think of her future alone. She knew she wanted to volunteer somewhere. Travel also was definitely on her mind now that this trip had gone so well.

There was guilt to deal with, no question, but she was coming to terms with all of that through reading about situations like hers and Don's. Her widowed friends also offered a lot of support and good advice. 'Life goes on' were three words she was hearing often.

Chapter Three

In early April, Libby took another major step on her own. She flew to visit Matthew and his family in Sydney, Australia where they were enjoying his temporary work placement.

The long flight provided time to relax and think about the changes in her life. She felt sad that Don could not be with her, but knew he was safe and well cared for at Serenity Palms. She gave herself permission to be excited about the adventure on which she was embarking and focused on the positive.

Libby was mobbed at the Sydney airport, smothered in hugs and kisses as her family greeted her. She was shocked by how much her grandchildren had grown in just two months.

"Grandma! G'day!" The teenagers greeted her with giggles. "We're so happy you are here." They beamed when Libby gushed over how they were growing up so quickly.

"What are they feeding you here? Or is it a special kind of sunshine that is making you both grow so much? My goodness, you look wonderful!"

"How was the flight, Mom? Did you manage to sleep?" Amy asked while Matthew took care of the luggage.

"I did! Thanks to the lovely first class upgrade you gifted me!" Libby said.

"The least we could do for you. It's such a long flight." Matthew said, when he returned with her bags, giving her another hug. "We're so glad you are here to experience our life 'down under' before we go back to Dragonfly Cove at the end of the month. The three months are flying by."

"We will be sad to leave here, but what makes it good is thinking about picking up our puppy", Kate said.

Amy said that Leslie, the dog breeder, had emailed photos of the newborn pup and a video of the whole litter after they were a week old.

"It's impossible not to be completely enchanted with the squirming, fluffy little blond bodies crawling over each other and snuggling with the mother", she said.

"Yeah! It's going to be so much fun to have a dog when we get home. But we do love it here, Grandma! Wait until you see what it is like." Jack said.

"And don't worry! We won't wear you out," Kate said, "Mom said we had to leave time for you to relax."

"And to bake with us!" Jack added. The grandchildren had spent a great deal of time in Libby's kitchen through the years and it was a treasured pastime. Libby's baking expertise was well known amongst her friends and relatives. She was delighted when she first discovered both Jack and Kate loved to work in the kitchen with her.

Libby grinned at his enthusiasm and tousled his hair. "Of course, we will bake! I bet I know what your first request will be."

"Grandma's Secret Surprise Special Cookies!!!" They both shouted. They had named them that when they were

A New Leash on Life

still in nursery school because often there was a surprise change to the recipe. Sometimes it was as simple as topping the cookie with a Smarties candy or changing the shape.

"How did I know you would say that?" Libby asked rhetorically. "And I have a new secret surprise in the recipe that I concocted just for this trip!"

Kate squealed with delight, while Jack began guessing what it might be.

Since Matthew's contract there was not long, he and Amy described to Libby their concerted efforts to immerse the family in the Australian way of life.

As they drove along the scenic highway, lined with beaches, to their home, Amy said "Even though it's winter here in the Southern Hemisphere, the weather is still warm, as you can see."

"We're at the beach with our friends all the time!" Kate told her.

"I've learned to surf!" Jack said proudly.

"That sounds like so much fun! And surfing! Wow, good for you! I hope you remember your sunscreen every time," Libby said, enjoying their enthusiasm.

Amy chuckled. "It's totally a way of life here, even when the sun is not so strong at this time of year."

Matthew nodded, adding, "We are never without it no matter what we are doing. It seems to be much more an issue here than it is in Florida."

A full itinerary was planned for Libby's visit. On day one, after an extensive driving tour around Sydney, she was impressed by the stunning natural beauty of the coastal landscape and the city's surroundings.

Matthew gave a running description as he drove. "It's such a unique blend of urban sophistication and coastal charm. We love the laid back, beach-oriented vibe just minutes from our neighbourhood and yet my office feels like it is in the middle of big city life. It's such a great lifestyle."

Amy told her about the ease of meeting neighbours and new friends and the comfortable sense of community they felt as soon as they arrived for their short stay.

In the early days after Libby's arrival, while she adjusted to the jet lag, Jack and Kate excitedly described the plans they had for her visit.

"Grandma, we've even booked a time at the zoo when you can hold a koala! You are going to love how soft they are!" Kate told her, showing photos on her phone. "I'm so happy you are here and can't wait to do it again with you!"

"But they will warn you about their sharp claws," Jack added. "Although we haven't yet had any problems."

"We wanted to go to Phillip Island with you to see penguins in the wild, but it's the wrong time of year," Kate explained. "So, we will have to be satisfied to take you to Sea Life at the Sydney Aquarium and ---"

Jack interrupted. "We've been waiting for you so we could do this! It looks so cool! We have to dress in subarctic snow gear and a boat ride takes us through a landscape of snow and ice just like where King Penguins actually live! The videos I've seen are awesome!"

"That does sound exciting!" Libby agreed.

"There's actually a special beach right in Sydney where Little Penguins are bred and protected." Kate said. "You can only get there by kayak and it depends on the weather and waves, so we were not sure if we would get to go while you are here. We did go one day when the weather was perfect and it was so fun. They are so tiny and adorable!"

"Well, it is obvious you are becoming penguin experts while you are here," Libby said. "That's not something you can do in Florida and I think that is awesome."

A New Leash on Life

With the children on school holiday, each day was filled with activity. Libby could see why they were loving living there in such beautiful surroundings. They went on road trips that took her to stunning golden beaches that stretched for miles, rugged cliffs dropping dramatically into the sea and verdant national parks.

Boat rides from busy Sydney harbour, bustling with ferries, sailboats and yachts provided stunning views of the iconic Sydney Harbour Bridge, world famous Sydney Opera House and the dramatic city skyline.

Hiking along the coastal paths provided breathtaking views over the Pacific. Beaches were busy with people surfing, swimming and relaxing.

"I can see why you all love it here with so much to do in these spectacular settings and lovely temperatures. Why would you ever want to be indoors? I thought Florida offered the perfect opportunities for outdoor activities, but I must admit this impresses me so much more. Compared to the flat terrain of Florida, everywhere you look here has such beauty."

Libby was also happy to see Kate and Jack still joined her in baking sessions with the same enthusiasm as always.

"I was afraid you might not want to do this now that you are growing up with your own busy lives," Libby said as they mixed ingredients and joyfully breathed in the aromas wafting from the oven.

"Never!" they said in unison.

In the second week of Libby's visit, Matthew was asked by his boss to remain for another three months.

That evening they had planned a feast of a shrimp and steak barbecue accompanied by Libby's new favorite salad, roasted pumpkin, goat cheese and macadamia nuts. The honey and balsamic dressing brought together the satisfying blend of flavors.

"This recipe is one Australian souvenir I am definitely taking home!" Libby told them.

Then, feeling comfortably full, they sat on the patio to discuss the news. "The work project is going really well, Mom. And to be honest, I don't have a choice," Matthew explained. He poured them each a glass of wine, hoping to soften the surprise of this sudden change in their plans.

A conversation with all the family revealed that Amy, Jack and Kate were excited to stay as well.

However, there was one very evident concern.

"But what about the pup? Can someone else take it and you arrange for another when you get home?" Libby asked, trying to disguise the note of hope in her voice. Somehow, she had a foreboding.

Matthew paled and looked down at the patio tiles for a moment. "Well Mom ... I was wondering if you would ..." His voice rose an octave as the rest of the words came rushing out in a run-on barrage. "... pick him up and keep him for us. It takes years to get on the list for a pup from Leslie, the breeder. She is so respected and has long waiting lists. We don't want to lose this opportunity."

Libby's jaw dropped, as the reality of what he was saying sunk in when he added, "It will just be for three months."

She looked at him in amazement. Her palms became moist. "You have got to be kidding! I have two cats. Who, as you know very well, rule our house. I've never had a dog."

Four sets of eyes were locked on her. Matthew and Amy were one thing, but Libby could never deny anything to Jack and Kate, who owned her heart.

"Well, it looks like I don't have any choice. I know what

A New Leash on Life

your dad would have said," she muttered, and was immediately overwhelmed with hugs and squeals of delight. They knew what their dear grandfather would have said too.

"The pick-up date is on the Saturday, two weeks after you get home," Matthew said in a quiet voice. "I'm so grateful to you, Mom. I will call Leslie and explain."

Libby's thoughts on the flight home were very different than the flight there. Although she always was happy to help out her family, this was not something she had ever considered ... a puppy in her life!

What was she getting herself into, she wondered, more than once. Feelings of doubt and concern kept entering her thoughts.

She knew how much work dogs, especially young ones, were from friends who had gone through the experience. Could she put up with the barking and whining she had heard about from others? The potty training? The chewing? All the walks whether she felt like it or not?

She was a cat person through and through. They were so easy to care for and so independent and loving ... just the right combination.

After mulling everything over and then over again, she finally put her anxieties aside. She could do it. She was coping with all the other changes in her life and she would cope with this one too. After all, the time will fly by ... or will it?

Chapter Four

The two weeks after she returned home were chaotic.

An immediate phone call to Leslie, to talk about the pup, was Libby's first order of business. She had a lot of questions. Matthew had emailed Leslie and explained that his mother was going to take the pup until their return.

Libby talked with her dog owner friends and read up on puppy raising online and watched endless videos about yellow Labs. She also spent a lot of time parked by the dog park, and feeling like a stalker, watching the interactions of so many different breeds and the non-stop activity.

Now, two weeks plus a day after Libby's return from Australia, it was all go.

※ ※
※ ※

Libby shook her head in disbelief one more time.

She had popped open the back of her mid-size SUV to place a bag of groceries beside the dog carrier, dog crate, dog

A New Leash on Life

bed, dog food, dog dishes, dog collar, harness and 6-foot leather leash, dog toys and a box of doggie poop bags.

With a wry grin, she brushed a hand over her short, silvery hair and stared at everything purchased that morning.

Marge, standing beside her, patted her shoulder. "Yup. That looks like someone about to become a dog owner. Even if it is a reluctant one. I tell you, having a parrot for a pet is a much simpler undertaking."

Libby laughed. "I hear you! I bet preparing for Einstein's arrival was not nearly as complicated."

"Definitely not. But then it was so many years ago I hardly can recall everything I needed to do. He was the replacement for my ex-husband after our divorce and I was excited to be having a voice I wanted to hear come and live with me. If you get my drift."

Libby chuckled. "I do remember that. Do you think you got more of a voice than you counted on?"

Marge laughed in return. "Einstein certainly is a blabbermouth but I love him for it. There was way more to learn about African Grey Parrots than I bargained for, but it's been so much fun. And still is. You are going to find the same thing with a new pup ...even if it is just temporary."

"It's been a whirlwind of a journey these past two weeks, that's for sure," Libby said as they drove over to her house. "Who would ever have predicted this for me? I must be crazy."

Marge's phone rang. "That's my sister in New York and I've been expecting her call. I'll go in the back yard to take it and you put your feet up for a few minutes. You can use the rest."

Libby had to admit she was glad to sit for a few minutes. It would give her some time to stop sounding so worried and paranoid about taking the pup. Both cats leapt onto her lap for some attention and her mind slipped back into the memories of the past few weeks.

A month before, her life felt somewhat organized and predictable in many new ways. It wasn't exactly the way she wanted her life to be, with many lonely moments without Don and new schedules for her to discover, but she had an idea of how it would be. Now a new challenge was beginning and she wondered if she was up to the task. Taking in a pup? It would certainly be part of her rewirement project.

Chapter Five

Looking flushed, Marge returned from taking her phone call. "Whoops! Sorry that took longer than I expected. We hadn't talked in ages and, with the crazy life she leads, I've got to take her calls when they come."

"I hope everything is okay," Libby said.

"No problems. Just good things actually ... new grandkids on the way for her! But let's get back to our adventure here."

"Yes, let's do this, Marge. It's going to be a scorcher today so we will want to be back home in our air-conditioned splendour the sooner the better. Let's get all this paraphernalia into the house and then make the pickup. Thanks for the support."

Marge chuckled. "Libby, even though that sounds like we're going to a parcel depot or a drug dealer, I believe you are ready for what lies ahead. And I also believe you are going to be pleasantly surprised with this new addition to your life. So please try to stop all that anxiety I hear coming from you."

Libby shrugged. "Tell that to the cats. And remember, I'm only going to be a temporary dog owner ... with a capital T. I'm just doing this to help the kids. In three months, all of this will be gone."

Max and Mimi had welcomed them at the side entrance door from the garage. Now they stood guard as they watched all the boxes coming into the house. Libby knew they were going to love those cartons once they were emptied.

"These two are like the official greeters at Walmart," Marge joked as she scratched each cat's head and smiled at the chorus of loud purring.

The cats had free run everywhere, including outdoors. It had never been a problem. When Don had closed in the carport eight years earlier, after one too many hurricanes, he built an elaborate climbing area for the cats which they loved and accessed through a cat door.

"I guess the puppy will learn about that cat door soon enough," Marge said. "Although he won't fit for very long. Those Labs get big!"

Libby nodded. "Another thing to worry about for a while. He will fit for the time he is here. And he will be safe in the garage. Nowhere else to go when it's closed up."

In her classic 1950's Florida bungalow, besides the garage entrance, the front door led directly into the living room. A dining area off the kitchen, three bedrooms and two bathrooms completed the layout and the sliding patio doors led to a screened lanai and pool. Now Libby had some concerns about the pup running out the front door.

"I might have to put up a temporary fence in the front, until the pup goes to Matthew's family," she suggested to Marge. "What do you think?"

"That could be a problem," Marge agreed.

A New Leash on Life

Libby stared at the door for a moment. "I'll come up with some solution."

The cats explored each item as it was brought into the house. Libby reminded them she had explained all of this to them, as they rubbed against her legs and eyed all the new acquisitions with suspicion.

They were in and out of every box as it was emptied.

"I'm going to leave a few of these cartons here for a while for them to enjoy," Libby said when Marge began breaking them down.

Marge helped organize where the crate would go. In the living room there was a bookcase next to the space and the top row was filled with books about puppies and dogs.

"You've been doing some extensive research," Marge observed.

"Got that right," Libby agreed. "I had to order the books online as Beach Reads is still closed since Vrai's tragic passing. The barista at Beachside Brews said she hasn't seen anyone there." She didn't bother to mention the books she'd purchased online were ones she'd already ordered and paid for through Beach Reads. It wasn't important in light of everything that had happened.

Marge lowered her eyes. "I haven't been to the store since Vrai died and I feel terrible about that. I didn't realize it was still closed. Actually, I have a book order of new mysteries there that Vrai had recommended and I've already paid for. I should have at least sent a note to her sister but I kept planning to drop by with something and pick up my books. How is she doing? Her name is Leola?"

"Yes, but I haven't spoken to Leola since Vrai died. I left an orchid plant with a note at Leola's little house, which is right beside Vrai's in the same park, which also must be difficult. Vrai was such a lovely part of our community here and her death was a terrible shock. She was a special person in my life and felt like family."

They both closed their eyes and shook their heads in sympathy. It was so difficult to find words for such a tragic situation.

Libby continued. "Leslie told me that Leola and Vrai had each reserved a dog and Leola is going to take both of them. She's going to have her hands full."

"Brave soul! But I understand why she would. It's very sweet of her."

"I think so too," Libby agreed. "One of them will always be Vrai's pup. Breaks my heart. I wonder when the store will re-open, if ever."

"It will be such a loss if it closes. Perhaps someone else will buy it," Marge said. Then she became quiet before changing the subject.

"How long will it be before the pups can have playdates?"

"In two more months," Libby said. "Once their shots have kicked in. From what I've read and been told, I'm going to be pretty busy during that time … kinda like having a baby again. Schedules, naps, and potty training … "

She paused and rolled her eyes. "My gosh! What have I gotten myself into?"

Marge chuckled. "You will be fine … but busy … and of course, the cats will no doubt be demanding some extra attention. I can't wait to hear how they react to this interloper."

Libby sighed and tried to ignore the knot of anxiety in her stomach. "Let's go! We will soon find out."

Chapter Six

The big wraparound porch surrounding Leslie's cheerful yellow house was filled with happily chatting future dog owners. The lawn was neatly mowed, the gardens edged and a variety of dog toys were organized in one corner on the grass.

"Clearly a very organized person lives here," Marge commented to Libby. They crossed the spacious fenced yard that was bordered by stately, long-established Live Oak trees and appreciated the shade they offered.

Libby was first up the stairs to the verandah to join the others. She smiled tentatively, hoping she appeared somewhat excited. How embarrassing it would be to have everyone there sense her reluctance to pick up a puppy. Even if it was for someone else.

"Talk about feeling weird," she muttered to Marge, who gave her a poke.

Libby, shifted the cookie tin filled with her caramel-swirled brownies that she'd brought to leave with Leslie. She fought off a nervous shiver. It was just a puppy she was going to hold for crying out loud, not a nuclear bomb.

"I just don't know how I'm going to pull this off," she muttered to Marge, who gave her a hard stare.

Any reassurance Marge might've offered was interrupted by the rapid approach of a tall thirty-something woman with blondish hair pulled up into a messy, slightly greasy bun. She held two puppies, one in each arm, and looked like she was fleeing a nightmare, not cuddling a dream team.

Libby's heart sank as recognition hit. She slapped a hand over her mouth. Leola—or Leo, as everyone calls her. Vrai's sister. And she'd just made such an insensitive remark to Marge. Like anything Libby was worried about could remotely compare to what Leo was going through.

"Busted," she said weakly, offering Leo what she was sure was the lamest smile of all times. "I'm a very reluctant dog owner."

Marge nervously chuckled.

Leo on the other hand looked . . . almost relieved or something. "I hear you," she said, looking from small dog to small dog nestled in her arms.

"Leo," Libby said. "You're Vrai's sister."

"And you're Libby. Libby M-Moore." It sounded as if Leo was choking, and Libby, knowing all too well how empty platitudes were, waited for her to continue rather than saying something just for the sake of filling the silence.

"I have books for you," Leo said finally. "They've been in for a while. I should've called." Her eyes widened and she winced. "You needed them for—"

Libby, realizing the poor girl had made the connection between the plethora of puppy training books and today's meet up, shook her head earnestly. "Of course you didn't call. I never expected you would with everything going on."

A New Leash on Life

"Well, I will get them to you."

"Anytime—or no time. Seriously, I will pick them up."

The two yellow bundles snuggled in Leo's arms wiggled and started to whine.

Relief flooded Leo's face and Libby thought she knew why. The puppies had given her an easy exit line.

"I better get these guys home," Leo said, proving Libby correct, "but I'll call you with a time that you can come pick up your books."

Libby nodded, then felt confused when Leo muttered "*Fine*," a bit scathingly or something. It didn't fit with their conversation.

"That is to say, I mean . . . I will call *this* week." Leo's smile was obviously forced, not that Libby blamed her one bit. She stepped back, allowing another woman and man with their own new furry bundle in tow, to move down the steps. And before she could reassure Leo again that she was in no hurry for the books, Leo was down the steps and striding across the yard.

Libby stared after Leo for a moment, feeling a heaviness in her heart for the young woman. She was dealing with such unexpected tragedy. The burden of loss and the challenge of moving forward would be immense. She promised herself to offer more support to Leo. The puppies would be great conversation starters.

Then she turned back to Marge. "You didn't mention the mysteries you ordered in."

Marge shook her head and, with a sad expression, waved her hand. "She's got enough on her plate for now. My books will keep."

One by one, happy people left with new floppy-eared additions to their families.

Finally, it was Libby's turn to pick up Matthew's pup. Leslie had carefully selected one she felt would be perfect for the family. Libby noted Leslie looked a little bleary-eyed as she and Marge entered the room, but her characteristic bright smile was back as she greeted them.

"Welcome to your very exciting day! Oh my gosh, what is this?" Leslie asked as Libby handed her the tin of brownies.

"Ohhh, thanks so much!" Leslie's eyes lit up as she lifted the lid. "These will be enjoyed to the fullest!"

"I guess this is a pretty emotional day for you," Libby said, "with all of your sweet little babies leaving the nest. This is just a little something for when you take a break."

"Got that right, I'm an emotional wreck by the end of this day. Thanks for being so thoughtful. I will savor these for sure," Leslie said as she peeked inside the container again.

Then she continued. "With every litter I swear I'm not going to lose control as I say goodbye to each pup. Never works! They are all such sweeties. You've come at a good time. It's quiet for the moment. Last time I looked your little guy was snoozing."

"Well, remember, he's not really mine. I'm just being Grandma until Matthew gets home in three months."

Leslie gave her a cryptic smile and winked at Marge. "Yeah, we will see about that."

Libby brushed off the comment, knowing she would never keep the dog forever. Jack and Kate had already made a schedule of when they could Facetime with her and "their" pup. Their excitement had not lessened in any way.

"I'll merely be the surrogate caregiver," Libby persisted.

A New Leash on Life

Leslie handed her a notebook and explained it had all the Vet's information and her own observation notes made daily on the pup's progress. "There are also links to a whole bunch of articles, resources, websites and books. But I've shared a lot of that with you already these last two weeks."

"I really appreciate all you have done and all the time you've given me convincing me I could handle this unexpected change in my life."

"Your pup ... oops, I mean Jack and Kate's pup ... is a feisty little guy with lots of energy but a very sweet disposition. He loves to cuddle. He will test you but you will love him anyway. I promise!"

"Yikes, that's just what I need ... feisty! Well, perhaps Mimi and Max will put him in his place."

Leslie laughed and nudged Libby. "Two cats, eh? That's going to make it even more fun!"

Libby laughed too. "Hey, we can never have too much fun in our lives. How about introducing me to my grandpup now?"

Leslie hesitated, then spoke with assurance. "I don't say this to everyone, but I feel he has an innate ability to sense troubled feelings in humans. To my amazement I have noticed this several times since he was born. There is something about the calm he assumes at the right times. Don't get me wrong, he still has crazy puppy attacks but in his own way he is quite special. Of that I have no doubt and I've closely observed a lot of puppies."

Libby was intrigued by this and Marge looked equally puzzled. Leslie ended the conversation with this. "I will be interested to see what you think in a few weeks. Don't worry. It's a good thing ...a very good thing. Okay, now let's put this little guy in your arms."

Leslie reached in and gently gave the sleeping pup a

little shake. His eyelids fluttered drowsily as the tiny bundle stirred. The puppy's nose twitched and a soft whimper greeted Leslie as she folded him into her arms.

"Meet the new member of your family, Libby. Truly a bundle of joy!"

Libby reached out somewhat awkwardly and stroked the pup's back. Its little tail began to wag with a newfound energy as Leslie tenderly passed him over.

From the moment Libby held the golden ball of fluff in her arms and his soulful brown eyes met hers, she was overcome with mixed feelings.

"Oh, he is adorable," Libby murmured, feeling a strong surge of unexpected affection. Still groggy, the pup nestled under her chin, the soft fur feeling like silk.

Leslie smiled warmly. She watched that reaction happen time and again as each pup went off to a new owner. In spite of Libby's previously expressed misgivings, Leslie's years of experience as a breeder left no doubt what her reaction eventually would be.

Leslie handed a grinning Marge a green rubber bone that squeaked and a small, crumpled blanket. "The pup has used these with his siblings and the scent will help him to feel more secure in his new surroundings."

"You've thought of everything," Libby complimented Leslie. "Thank you so much. And have a great time in Italy! I heard via the grapevine that you are heading off on your own adventure." She followed that with an exaggerated wink. The rumor mill had been busy with news about a handsome Italian being the main reason for Leslie's trip.

Leslie flashed a wide smile and Libby thought she noticed a bit of a blush, as she nodded. "Yes, it should be fun! Don't forget my friend Emily will be around to answer any questions or get you whatever help you need. I don't expect there will be anything but you never know. Her number is in the notebook."

"Arrivederci!" Libby and Marge called as they walked to the car, with Libby cradling a fluffy bundle.

Chapter Seven

As Marge drove, Libby held the pup close to her chest and found herself murmuring sweetly to him. His soft whimper and dark expressive eyes that conveyed sweetness and trust filled her with surprising emotions.

Out of the blue, Libby whispered, "Chance. That's what I'm naming him. I suddenly feel he is giving me a chance to be happy again."

"I think you have the right to do just that. I'm happy you are feeling this."

Libby nodded. "So am I ... and totally shocked at my instant reaction."

Marge looked over and gave the pup's head a gentle rub. "He's quite irresistible."

Libby spoke softly but firmly, looking lovingly at the pup. "If the kids don't like the name, they can change it when he goes to live with them. But while he's with me, he is Chance."

Marge nodded. She could see a look of peace in Libby's eyes.

A New Leash on Life

The transition with the cats was chaotic that first day. Chance was completely oblivious to the fact that the cats resented his presence and his unending attempts to play with them. Libby had never heard such hissing and yowling from her sweet felines as they dashed to perch atop the couch. The pup simply thought it was a great game.

While they were out of his reach, Chance sniffed the air with curiosity, his tail wagging at warp speed. The cats glared back. Max arched his back and puffed up his silvery fur, looking fierce as a deep growl emanated from him. Mimi calmed down but remained watchful and unblinking.

When Chance realized his efforts to climb up on the sofa were fruitless, he explored the rest of the room. Taking hesitant steps, he sniffed and poked his way around the chairs and coffee table.

Little by little, Libby steered him towards his crate. Without any apprehension, he spent some time examining the soft bed and toys waiting for him there. Marge had placed the blanket from Leslie in the crate already and Chance rubbed his face in it as if recognizing the familiarity.

Next, Libby followed him around the room while Marge sat on the couch and reassured Mimi and Max. The latter, who by this time had unpuffed himself, but was definitely not relaxed.

Once Chance meandered into the kitchen the cats leapt to the floor and peered through the archway making certain he did not go near their food. Libby stayed close to him, watching for a telltale puddle to appear.

"Oh, don't worry, you two," Libby reassured the cats, pointing to the counter. "Your food is safely up here for now." They leapt up on the marble-topped island as Chance made a beeline to try to play with them again.

The doors to the other rooms were closed to keep the exploration limited for his first day. Libby gently guided Chance to his new water bowl and he lapped up a small amount.

After a few minutes, with the cats now on the counter, still watching Chance's every move, Libby put a leash on his collar and led him outside to the carefully prepared potty place. This exercise took four attempts as the pup stopped to investigate everything.

Each time there was no result Libby brought him to his crate, spoke softly and positively to him, and waited a few minutes before trying again.

The constant need to monitor Chance's every move reminded Libby of having a toddler back in her life.

"Marge, I'm beginning to realize how demanding this is going to be. I better cancel tennis for the next few weeks."

"Your work is cut out for you here, for sure. Why don't you get a sub at tennis for this week and then, if you feel Chance is settling in after that, I'll come over here and puppysit while you go to your games. I noticed we have a different schedule for this month."

"Good plan and so nice of you! You know Barb and Brian next door always look after the cats when I'm away long term. But I wouldn't ask them to take on a pup. Let's see how it goes."

Then her face crumpled with worry. "Oh man, I didn't even think about my weekly hikes. I can't ask you to come over for that. Sometimes I'm gone for hours and besides half the time you are with me."

"Well," Marge reminded her, "before you know it the three months will be over and Chance will go to Matthew's. The time will fly by."

A New Leash on Life

Libby nodded. "In fact, it's already just two and a half months to go."

They sat quietly for a minute. Chance was settled happily in Libby's arms, licking her hand as she stroked his chest.

Libby's face brightened. "I just had a brainwave! I've seen ads for carriers for pups ... backpacks ... and other options. I'm going to look into one of those. It would mean I can take Chance hiking with me."

"Great idea," Marge replied, wondering if Libby had even heard her reminder about Matthew's family returning. "With all the dogs we already have going along in our group, you know how welcome the pup would be. Now I'm getting excited about that!"

"How about the nursery out in the lanai? I wonder what Chance will think of that?" Marge was referring to the screened porch leading to the pool where Libby and Don had begun raising monarch butterflies years ago.

There were four mesh enclosures to discourage the cats from getting curious. Inside each were little pots with milkweed which the caterpillars fed on until they went into the larva stage. Libby also had large milkweed plants in the garden to supplement their appetites.

"This was really Don's project and I'm trying my best to keep it going," Libby said. "It's a pleasure to see a beautiful monarch emerge from its chrysalis. After just a few hours they are ready to fly out and be free. They feed on the milkweed plants in the garden and I collect eggs they lay there and the process starts all over again."

"It's such a good thing to do! Looks to me like you are handling it just fine. I see lots of potential beauties about to pop!"

"Yup, Don had everything so well organized and I thank

him every day for that," Libby murmured. "I won't bring the pup into this area until he's more mature. The cats really don't pay any attention to all of this, so hopefully he won't either."

"That sounds like a good plan. Well, everything seems under control, so I'm heading home. Have fun for the rest of the day!" Marge said as she gave Libby a hug.

"Thank you for all your help today. I really appreciate it," Libby said, as she picked up a box from the table and handed it to Marge. "I was out doing a few errands earlier and stopped by your favorite place."

"Sticky Buns Bakery! Those cinnamon buns are my addiction and you know it! Thanks! And not necessary, at all ... but thanks! Einstein will be delighted to have a taste!"

"I might have bought a couple for myself too," Libby said with a grin. "You know, I've never made them because Don was not a fan of cinnamon. I guess I never will because no one could bake them better than these!"

They hugged again and Libby waved goodbye as Marge backed her car out of the driveway.

Chapter Eight

Chance seemed to be happy with his comfy nest in the crate. He flopped down and fell asleep immediately after a short playtime. The blanket Leslie had given them from her place was in there and he nestled his face right into it.

Libby was shocked to find herself tearing up as she watched him peacefully asleep. "The innocence of a sleeping baby," she murmured to herself.

The instant affection she felt for the pup continued to surprise her.

She was eager to take Chance over to visit with Don but knew it would be best to wait until he was a bit older. Certainly, she had to wait until he was 16 weeks before he could socialize with other dogs. Then he would be fully vaccinated.

Right about that time, Matthew and family would be back, she suddenly realized. Then she banished the thought.

At the end of the day, after countless trips to go potty and a few attempts at walks around the yard along with numerous play and cuddle sessions, Libby found herself as exhausted as Chance.

That night, after a successful final visit outside, Libby kissed the top of his silky, golden head as Chance settled into his bed. She closed the door to his crate, turned off the lights and went into her bedroom.

Mimi and Max were already in their favorite spots on the bed, waiting for her to join them.

It wasn't long before the whimpering began. And it did not stop. The soft, plaintive sound tugged at her heartstrings.

Libby pulled a pillow over her head, determined to ignore it. Everyone knew this was to be expected but it was more difficult than she imagined it would be.

After tossing and turning for an hour, Libby finally gave in and carried the pup in the crate to the bedroom. She sat next to it, caressing Chance and reassuring him, until he slipped into a deep sleep.

At midnight and again at 5 a.m., Chance was wide awake and Libby sighed resignedly each time as she stepped into her flipflops. Slipping on his leash as she cradled him to the back door, they went to the potty place.

Sticking to the task at hand, Libby did not let Chance linger on the way. In the middle of the night these visits were strictly business. There would be plenty of time to smell the flowers during the day she told him.

After each unsuccessful attempt, he went straight back into his crate and by the third time, he seemed to have the idea. By morning, Libby was not well rested but Chance was ready to play.

And so the days progressed.

Chance awoke in the mornings with seemingly boundless energy, his dark eyes sparkling with curiosity. His excited response to seeing Libby made her feel so loved and important to him, she could not help but begin her day with joy.

And every so often she couldn't help think of Vrai's sister Leo, who had indeed called Libby about the books, which Libby picked up, not mentioning the repeats. She'd give the new copies to Jack and Kate. And what she hoped every time the bookseller popped into mind was that her two little dogs were bringing joy back to her, as well.

Libby had instantly felt a connection to Leo that day on the porch at Leslie's. She recognized the grief, although very different from hers, that Leo was coping with. She made a promise to herself then to keep in closer touch and hopefully at some point they could have a conversation about it. She had come to realize that no one understood how all-consuming grief could be, unless they had experienced it and how talking about it was often a relief.

Chapter Nine

F or a few more days, Max and Mimi continued to react with hisses and arched backs, beating hasty retreats, whenever the pup bounced over to them. But gradually, when Chance was sleeping, they approached the crate, sniffing all around.

Libby had reorganized things and ordered a second crate, so there was now one in the living room and one in her bedroom.

Mimi was the first to give in to Chance's awkward playful advances. They were soon running circles around each other and through the house. Max assumed a haughty posture and remained aloof from a higher perch. He observed for several days before he cautiously joined in.

Chance chased after them, full of energy and enthusiasm. To him it was all a game. A few swipes with their paws were no deterrence and Libby observed that they didn't seem to want to use their sharp claws.

Libby had not laughed so much in years as she watched the playful chases that often evolved into gentle wrestling.

She could see the cats begin to enjoy this newfound activity becoming part of their daily routine.

The playtimes were brief at first as Chance was soon exhausted and flopped asleep at the most unpredictable moment. The first time Libby came upon the three of them snuggled together sleeping, she took photos and texted them off to Australia.

She loved the messages she received back with her family surprised and delighted that Chance was being so well accepted.

"We think he loves living with you, Grandma! Thank you for being so good to him."

"He's just so, so, so cute," Kate kept repeating. "I can't wait to cuddle him when we get back."

Libby had a brief pause wondering how she would feel about Chance moving to Matthew's. It was still almost two months off she reminded herself and put the thought out of her mind. Again.

Libby stuck to a strict schedule with his crate training. Leslie had included detailed instructions, easy to follow, in the information she had given to her. She was surprised at how effective it was. Chance showed no hesitation going into the crate and Libby could see it was a safe, comfortable place for him.

She had heard from some friends how pups were always chewing shoes and other items lying around and could see how the crate prevented that. She was thankful that it never seemed to be necessary to discipline Chance. Although they did have to have a few conversations about the odd puddle.

If that was the worst she had to deal with, Libby felt blessed.

Jack and Kate continued to FaceTime regularly and

cooed and giggled as Libby held Chance up to the camera. She followed him around with the phone so the kids could see what sort of mischief he was up to with his toys. Matthew and Amy joined in and agreed the pup was adorable. They laughed uproariously watching him chase the cats.

Chapter Ten

Two months flew by.

Libby was surprised at how quickly Chance was changing. He was becoming less awkward as his size and weight increased. He was catching on to playing fetch with his ball but preferred to run away with it instead of returning it. Libby laughed as she chased him around the house.

It dawned on her that all those fears she had were vanishing.

During that time Libby could see he was happy in his home and a friendship continued to develop with the cats. When he was out of his crate, one or both of the cats might decide to enjoy a snooze in there.

Libby chuckled whenever she discovered them all cuddled together now that Chance was spending more time out of his crate. His accidents were happening less often and Libby patted herself on the back for being so consistent with his training. *Just like Matthew's potty training days*, she would chuckle.

While she waited for his full vaccinations, Libby gradually introduced Chance to the pool. Part of Libby's daily routine during the hot humid weather was to swim laps. Chance took to water as she read Labs would and after a few days he was able to swim to the steps when she let him go, his little legs paddling and splashing. Pool time soon became an exciting part of his day.

It wasn't long before he would stand eagerly by the edge of the pool, his quickly-growing paws dancing in place, and wait for Libby to say "jump". With his ears perked up and body wiggling with excitement, as he hit the water he began splashing with exhilaration.

"It's pure puppy joy!" Libby described to everyone who would listen.

She couldn't wait to see how he responded to the beach when the time was right to take him there.

His tail wagged at warp speed when Marge came over. Even more so when she brought her visiting grandchildren along. All of Libby's tennis friends popped by to meet him and Chance responded well to the attention. He loved to chew on fingers and his puppy teeth were sharp and beginning to fall out, so Libby kept a soft toy handy to distract him.

Libby felt pleased with the way she had become comfortable training Chance. Her anxieties had all disappeared. Since she was accustomed to vacuuming up cat hair every day, the addition of Chance's golden fluff was not a big deal.

There was no question how very much she loved him but she never stopped reminding herself that he would soon leave her. She was well aware it would be a wrench and she would miss his constant companionship. She kept repeating she had just signed up for temporary guardianship.

Doctor Sawyer commented on how well behaved he

A New Leash on Life

was when they went for Chance's shots. Leslie was right. She had noticed the pup reacted gently with people and Libby saw this too, compared to some she saw who were hyper and liked to jump at everyone.

The training was going well according to the observations of some of the other owners of pups from the litter who she bumped into in their little community.

Now that they were all vaccinated, there was often a gathering at the dog park in the late afternoon as temperatures cooled.

The first time Libby ventured to the park with Chance after week 16, she noticed other yellow Lab pups that looked just like him. She knew Emily from Barks and Brews where she and Don had often popped in with Jack and Kate when they were small, as the kids enjoyed kicking a soccer ball around the big play area there.

"Hey Emily, how are you and your pup doing? Easy to tell these sweeties are from the same litter!" Libby said.

"Great to see you, Libby. You haven't needed to call for help so I assume you and your new buddy have been getting on well."

"We really have. This has been so much easier than I imagined and he's an incredibly good little guy. His name is Chance."

Emily gestured to an attractive woman standing with her. "Meet Nora. As you can see, she has one of the pups from our litter too."

Nora smiled brightly. "Hi, nice to meet you! That's Charlie who is roaring after the pups over there. He is the speediest little dog I've ever seen ... and a bit of a challenge, but sweet. But our training hasn't gone quite as easily as yours from the look of it."

Emily said, "And that's my Daisy trying to catch up with Chance."

The three women stood and chatted, laughing at the antics as the pups raced around. They all agreed they had found their pup highly food motivated.

"There's nothing like the offer of a you-know-what to get the right response," Emily said, as the others nodded.

"Leslie made that clear in the information she gave us and she was absolutely right. I believe **t r e a t** was the first word Chance recognized." She spelled it out so there would not be a frenzy with all the pups.

"Do you think they feel a connection?" Libby wondered. They compared how the eight weeks since pickup day had flown by. Each was as happy with their pup as Libby was with Chance.

"I'm thinking about talking to Hank about puppy obedience lessons," Libby said. "I know Chance does what he is told in the house but I'm a bit nervous about being out in public. I want to make sure I train him properly for my son and his family. What do you think?"

"That's a good idea," Emily said as Nora nodded. "It certainly can't hurt. Hank may enjoy looking a little bizarre, but he has an excellent reputation and his classes are often sold out. I know Charlie and I still have some work to do."

"Well, I may not be able to get a booking right away after hearing how busy he is. I'll only have Chance for another month and then he will go to my son's family and I will just be the grandmother."

"I'd forgotten about that," Emily said. "Wow, how difficult will that be for you?"

Libby swallowed the lump in her throat. "I'm not going to pretend it will be easy. I am far more attached to this little darling than I ever imagined I would be. I'll just have to deal with it."

She tried to ignore the sickening feeling that gripped her whenever she talked about Chance leaving.

"And I'm sure you will see him often. Then perhaps you will get another pup! How about that?" Nora asked.

Libby shrugged and said, "I don't know about that. One day at a time."

Changing the subject, she asked Emily, "So, what's the latest on Leslie? Is she back from Italy? I figure if anyone knows it will be you."

Emily laughed. "You mean, do I have all the juicy details?"

Libby and Nora nodded, grinning broadly.

"Well as a matter of fact I have at least some of them. As you know by now, Leslie went off to meet a guy named Nico, whom she met online. I knew he was younger and was a bit worried about whether he was just a player. The good news is, he is a fabulous guy and crazy about Leslie and she is loving life in Italy."

"And apparently the feeling is mutual," Nora added, bouncing up and down and making them laugh. "How exciting is that? It may be true love!"

"Oh, I am so happy for her after that nasty split from her husband." Libby said.

"For sure! Les and I video chat several times a week and I've chatted with Nico. He's such a nice guy ... and gorgeous! Leslie loves his family too. It's going to be interesting to see what happens there but so far it is a happy story!"

Nora clapped her hands. "We can always use good news."

Emily asked how Don was doing and after a brief chat

about things at Serenity Palms, Libby explained that she was going to take Chance to meet him in the next day or two.

"Let me know how it goes! These Labs have a good reputation knowing when to be gentle. Everything should be fine. Please tell Don I send him a hug ...even though I know it won't mean anything to him, it means something to me. I miss him."

She leaned over and hugged Libby, as good friends do. Nora reached out to hug her as well and Libby appreciated the emotion they were all sharing.

Chapter Eleven

Several of Libby's friends were asking if she might get herself a dog once Matthew and family were home.

"Interesting question," she'd reply and promptly change the subject. The truth was she did not think she could go through training a puppy so soon again but the thought of an older rescue dog had entered her mind a few times.

The bigger question was how she would feel parting with Chance and just seeing him from time to time.

One day Matthew was the first on the video call, which was unusual. "Well, Mom, are you sitting down? Here's the news. We are staying here in Australia for another year."

Libby gulped ... and felt mixed emotions. "Oh dear, that's such a long time!"

"You can visit again ... as often as you like. We would love that. I know it's a surprise but we are all very happy to stay here. The kids have made good friends, as have Amy and I, and I love the job."

"I'm happy for you and I can see why you love it in that stunning country," Libby said. Her voice caught for a second and then she blurted, "Does that mean Chance is mine forever? Might you want him back after a year?"

Matthew chuckled and spoke tenderly. "Yes, he apparently is yours forever. After I explained to the kids that Chance would have to go into quarantine for six months if we brought him here, they understood it was not a good idea. Jack and Kate were the first to say that to take him away from you after a year would be cruel to you both. It must be serendipity because you both appear to love each other from all the cuddling we see!"

"Matty, he truly has been a godsend. That little bundle of love has brought happiness that was missing back into my life. My nights are lonely no more."

"Grandma, we still want to call once a week to watch him grow. Is that okay? It will be a long time before we get to have a dog."

Libby chuckled. "Of course, sweethearts. He will always belong to you too. And here I thought you were calling to see me!"

They all laughed, protesting that of course she was right.

🐾 🐾

After she hung up, Libby sat on the floor with Chance. She was surprised at her reaction to Matthew's news. Where was all the anxiety and concern she had originally harboured about owning a dog?

Chance had been playing with some toys and now crawled into her lap. She cuddled him even more closely than usual.

"Guess what, sweet boy," Libby murmured to him, her

A New Leash on Life

lips brushing his head with little kisses. "You are mine and I am yours, forever. In a thousand years, I would never have predicted this."

Chance lifted his head and covered her face with gentle licks as Libby wrinkled her nose and laughed.

As she sat there, she thought for a moment how she would miss Matthew and the family when they were so far away for so long. But she knew she would visit them again and that was exciting.

Quickly, her thoughts turned to Chance as she marveled at the joy he brought into her life. She had felt such loss with Don absent from her daily life. Unexpectedly, Chance brought laughter, warmth and an overwhelming sense of companionship back to her, all parts of the love that she had felt from Don.

As the pup drifted off to sleep on her lap, they stayed on the floor as Libby's thoughts centered on the changes being a dog owner had brought to her life. All of it was positive and welcome. In that moment, she realized that this little pup had stolen her heart completely. She couldn't imagine her life without him.

She happily had always been a creature of habit, a quality that suited her choice of profession as a librarian. After her retirement she often found herself missing the daily schedule that had been her life for so many years. She welcomed that back since Chance arrived and she felt revitalized. It brought more of a purpose to her days.

Max and Mimi were a constant source of affection but she had discovered a dog brings that in a very different and far more physical way. Playing with and walking Chance brought laughter as well as exercise, where playing with the cats was of a gentler manner. She did love those two felines and they were an important part of her life ... and Don's. It gave her great pleasure as she watched how Chance connected with them as the weeks went by.

As far as Libby was concerned, now that she knew she would not have to part with Chance, there were only positives that had come into her life since his arrival.

Who knew? She thought to herself. The bond they shared would only continue to grow and she felt a smile spread across her face before she drifted into a nap too.

She was wakened by Max meowing to let her know it was their dinner time. To her surprise, she had slept for a half hour. Chance bounced from her lap to chase Max and she went to the kitchen to fill the food bowls for all of her fur babies.

Before fixing herself a salad for dinner, she made a note to call her neighbour, Joe, and see if he could come and fence in the front yard. They had chatted about the job when she was walking with Chance one day, but she thought it did not make sense when the pup was going to Matthew's house soon. Now that scenario had completely changed.

Although the back yard was fenced around the pool, beyond that the open lawn backed onto a pond fringed by tall grasses. On a regular basis Libby and Don had spotted an alligator floating about. Occasionally, it would crawl onto one of the surrounding lawns to catch some mid-day sun.

She was not going to take any chances of tempting it with a puppy. Fencing the front yard meant she would not have to worry if Chance dashed out when she opened the front door. She knew she would never leave him out there alone.

Chapter Twelve

The day finally dawned when Libby prepared to take Chance to Serenity Palms for the first visit. She wrestled with conflicting feelings of happiness and anxiety. She felt nervous for Don and for Chance, hoping it would be a positive experience for both and that neither of them would feel frightened.

She had been telling Don all about the pup every day when she visited him. He had stared at many of the photos on Libby's phone, several times over. But each time it was as though it was the first. Don's conversation skills were becoming more and more limited but he would always ask whose dog it was and what its name was.

After a brief stroll around a garden filled with glorious Birds of Paradise in full orange and purple bloom, as soon as Chance did his business, they walked into the reception area. The caregivers were all aware of Chance's visit and excited to finally meet him.

Chance had been wearing his new harness for a few weeks now and had adjusted to it very well. Libby liked that it eliminated the pup pulling on the leash attached to his collar as they walked. Chance responded to the "heel" command and Libby felt he would be well behaved at the residence. At least she hoped so. Her pocketful of treats would help.

In the spacious entrance foyer, Chance bounced around and even, most unlike him, jumped up a few times as several people rushed to him. Libby knew this was the result of so many people greeting him with excitement. She watched as he got it out of his system before she took him down the hall to where the residents lived. That was one more reason she had booked him into puppy obedience classes that would start soon.

When she asked Chance to sit, he did so immediately ~ knowing a treat was coming. Libby chuckled as he looked at her expectantly, angelic, with his tail wagging non-stop.

She beamed as everyone fussed over him and told her what a sweet pup he was. After Chance had adjusted to all the commotion, she asked him to heel and they walked towards Don's room.

Libby could see people in the hallway react as they approached and knew she had to pause at the wheelchairs and walkers to allow those who wished to greet Chance. Their expressions of delight confirmed to her how disappointed they would have been if she simply walked by.

Chance was more controlled than he was in reception. It was as if he sensed these people needed him to be gentle. Their reactions surprised Libby. She was so focused on her own visit with Don, she had not given much thought to how a visit from Chance would be received by so many others.

Libby sensed the atmosphere in the hallway completely changing. There was laughter and some lively chatter amongst other visitors and residents. Happiness was in the air and it felt good. She could feel more involved interactions amongst the residents linger as they made their way along. The absence of the normal quiet, almost gloomy atmosphere felt good.

It seemed forever before they finally reached Don's room. A caregiver had gone ahead to make certain he was awake in his brown leather reclining chair by the picture window. The air conditioning rattled slightly and a subtle scent of lavender mingled with a hint of lemon greeted Libby as usual. Everything felt crisp and renewed.

Libby was grateful when the woman, whom she knew as Dorothy, assured her, "I will be with you as long as you like, Libby, in case you need some help."

Don did not react as Libby and Chance entered the room. She gently lifted his chin, knowing she would still only be greeted by a blank stare. Each day that was like a stab to her heart. She wanted to know he was still there somehow.

Libby leaned over and kissed his cheek. "Hi sweetheart, it's me ... your wife Libby."

There was still no reaction. She squeezed his shoulder tenderly.

Lifting up Chance and holding him near Don she said, "This is our new dog. His name is Chance. He came to live with us recently and is still a pup, just four months old." Her heart was pounding, filled with her desire for Don to respond in some way.

She longed to see there was something in life that could please him, rather than believing with great sorrow that he was living in a dark vacuum.

Dorothy came over and stroked Chance's head, cooing at how sweet and soft he was.

"Don, would you like to pet him?" Libby asked, knowing he would not understand.

Dorothy gently lifted his hand and helped him stroke the pup's back as he sat quietly in Libby's arms, staring intently at Don.

The corners of Don's mouth slowly moved ever so slightly upward. It wasn't exactly a hint of a smile, but it was something. When Dorothy let go of his hand, he continued to pet Chance hesitantly for a moment. Then he let his fingers rest in the satiny fur. His eyes never left the pup and Chance's dark brown eyes returned the gaze.

Libby felt tears well up and swallowed the lump in her throat. She spoke quietly to Don, telling him about the cats and how they were friends with Chance now.

As intensely as she watched his face for some understanding of her words, she saw none. But he did not remove his hand from Chance's back. After Libby looked at Dorothy for approval, which she gave with a nod, the pup remained calm and still as Libby sat him in Don's lap.

Don's other hand rested on his thigh. Chance moved his head toward it to give it a little lick.

Libby held her breath. Don's mouth turned upward just a little more and Libby's heart filled with joy. Dorothy handed her a tissue, as she wiped her own eyes.

Soon, Chance and Don both fell asleep. Don's hand remained on the pup's back.

Dorothy patted Libby's shoulder and whispered in her ear. "I would say this visit has been a great success. Bring Chance any time."

"I will bring him every time," Libby replied. "This turned out to be even better than I had hoped."

After half an hour, Chance wakened and Libby carefully picked him up. Don remained fast asleep so she tiptoed out. In the hallway, she put Chance down and once again he happily performed community service with residents and staff all the way to the exit door.

There was enough cloud cover in the otherwise bright blue sky to soften the glare of the sun, so Libby and Chance had a brisk walk along the pathways through the property before they drove home. It had been a long time since Libby had left Don's room feeling some happiness.

Unable to contain her excitement, she called Marge on the way home to report on the visit.

"That is awesome! I'm so happy for you! How wonderful that you could actually see some response from Don."

"It wasn't a great deal, and it might have been my imagination, but at least it felt like something," Libby said. "If I can bring him a bit of cheer with visits from Chance, that makes me feel like I'm contributing something to his dreary life. It was incredible to see how so many others loved giving Chance a pat or a rub. They need some dogs to visit there more often."

"For sure, that can be a good project" Marge agreed. "Let's go out for dinner tonight to celebrate and we can talk about that. Chance can come too, of course."

"Great idea! But Chance can stay home with Mimi and Max this evening. I've given him more than enough treats today. I would love to check out that new seafood restaurant by the harbour. Any interest?"

"You're on! I'm going for a mani/pedi at 5 p.m. so why don't I meet you there at 6:30."

"Sounds like a plan!"

Chapter Thirteen

Chance and Libby began visiting with Don every day. However, it soon became apparent that visits to Don included many more people. Libby could not bear to disappoint anyone by not stopping to let them pet Chance.

As soon as people realized Libby was in the hall with the pup, they left their rooms with walkers, canes and wheelchairs. Chance was the model of patience but Libby quickly saw how what should have been a 30-minute visit was turning into hours.

Doctor Anita Sherin, the head of the facility, met Libby as she arrived during the second week of her visits. After she bent down to give Chance a good back rub, she said, "Libby, I've been hearing what a wonderful gift you are bringing to Serenity Palms with the visits of your adorable pup. I'm so happy to meet him."

"I hope you are not finding it disruptive," Libby said.

"On the contrary. We are very aware of the positive benefits we see in all the patients. I want to thank you. However, we also see how demanding it is on you."

A New Leash on Life

Libby replied, "I'm happy to do it. I had no idea everyone would want an opportunity to pat him."

"Nor did we," Doctor Sherin said. "I have a proposition for you. If you agree, why don't we schedule you as a regular visitor with Chance three days a week at a certain time."

Libby protested, "But I visit my husband every day and always have Chance with me."

"Understood," Doctor Sherin replied. "You should continue to visit your husband as often as you wish. But you should not have the onus of visiting with everyone else each time. That is a lot. Your visits have given us an idea and we are going to reach out to other dog owners to visit as well. Of course, we will have the dogs carefully vetted to make certain they are as calm and quiet as Chance."

Libby listened carefully, weighing the doctor's words. "I agree, the visits are time consuming although they are extremely satisfying. I've been happy to do it. But it is a great idea to organize the community to visit with other pets. Let me know if I can help."

"I will do that. On the other days you plan to visit Don with Chance, call us first and we will arrange for Don to be outside or sitting quietly in another area. That way you can avoid the crowds ... if you get my drift."

Libby chuckled. "I understand and appreciate you helping me get organized with my visits. In fact, when the weather is right, it will be nice to take Don for a walk in his wheelchair with Chance coming along."

Doctor Sherin gently squeezed Libby's hand. "I know how difficult it is to have your spouse live apart from you. I hope you know how we admire the way you have adjusted."

"Thank you. I appreciate everything that is being done to make him comfortable here. The staff is wonderful."

Then she carried on to Don's room. As usual his head

was bowed and his eyes closed but, as soon as she placed Chance on his lap, his demeanor changed ever so slightly. His eyes opened and he placed his hand on the pup's back. Libby was certain he felt some sense of pleasure and that was good enough for her.

She always walked Chance before arriving so he was due for a nap before long. That worked well since Don frequently nodded off and the sight of Chance asleep on his lap warmed Libby's heart. She liked to think that somehow Don felt some peace with it too.

Life was shifting into a good rhythm. Now he was vaccinated, Libby would take Chance to her tennis games and attach his leash to a shady tree. He would poke around in the grass for a while but soon lie down and watch the world go by while she played for an hour and a half.

He accompanied her on hikes, sitting in his special backpack at first. Libby realized he would not need it for long at the rate he was growing. Even now he could walk for some time before getting tired, so she knew it would not be a problem.

The picket fence in the front yard was serving its purpose well. Libby could open the front door to greet guests or accept parcels and not worry about Chance dashing out, which he did from time to time.

She also had a vision of sweet peas along the fence and was excited to experiment. She strung wire down the pickets and planted packets of seeds which sprouted quickly. Since childhood, in her mother's garden, she would press her face into the fragrant blossoms and, in the past,

A New Leash on Life

had no success growing them. But she was certain the direction of the sun against the fence was just right for that flower and was thrilled when they bloomed abundantly.

When she was busy planting or weeding in the front flower beds, Chance would poke around, chasing butterflies and bugs. Often Mimi and Max would accompany him. Libby loved watching the three of them wander about the garden, roll in the grass and rub up to her for a scratch from time to time. These were peaceful times.

But one day, about a month after his vaccinations, the unthinkable happened.

Chapter Fourteen

It occurred so quickly, Libby could not process the shock at first.

On a Monday afternoon, she was sitting on the front porch after throwing Chance's ball around the yard. He sometimes became distracted by the butterflies around the lantanas, that were flush with brilliant pink and yellow blooms, and followed them as they fluttered past him. Then Mimi teased him into chasing her. His playful, sometimes clumsy, bounces were infectious and Libby couldn't help laughing,

Happy to have a rest, Libby sat on a wicker porch chair and chuckled at the antics of her pets. Max hopped up on her lap, content to have her to himself for a few minutes.

A white van with Pete's Plumbing written on the side parked in front of the house and a young man gave Libby a cheery wave. "Dad tells me you may have to start building an ark!"

"Not quite, but I was beginning to worry," Libby replied. "Your father told me he was slammed with work so I'm glad to see you drop by so quickly."

A New Leash on Life

"No rest for the weary, Mrs. Moore. You're a special customer so we found the time," Pete Junior said, flashing a big smile that was accompanied by a wink.

As a boy, Don had played on the same softball team as Pete Jackson and they had been friends since high school. Libby had taught Pete Jr. in elementary school. Dragonfly Cove was that sort of community where friends were always doing favors for friends.

"It sounds like a quick fix."

Libby checked to make sure the gate was properly latched. Chance was busy with Mimi. She left the front door open as she led Pete Jr. inside to the kitchen, as she would just be a minute. Max ran in with her.

The kitchen floor was covered with towels and water was dripping out from the cupboard under the sink.

"The problem seems to be where the water pipe comes into the house. I tried to shut it off but, as you can see, wasn't successful. I'll gather up these towels and get them out of your way."

She scooped them up and wrung them out in the sink, before putting them in a plastic basket which she placed on the counter.

"I'll take it from here, Mrs. Moore. No worries."

"Great! I'll be out front with the dog."

She closed the door as she went back out to the porch. Mimi was pacing the path from the gate to the house. Chance was nowhere to be seen. Libby called him and looked over to the thick growth of shrubs in the side garden where he often liked to investigate.

There was no response. That was unusual. Chance always came flying to her when called.

Trying to still the growing fear in her throat, she realized her voice was sounding increasingly alarmed as she looked everywhere. The pup was definitely not there. Then she went to the gate and saw that it was not completely latched. But she had closed it herself after Pete Jr. came through. She knew she had double checked it.

Libby quickly went out onto the street, still calling. To no avail.

Pete Jr. came out of the house and asked if everything was all right. "I could hear you calling Chance. Have you got him?"

In a trembling voice, Libby said, "No. And I just saw that the gate was not completely latched although I was positive I did close it properly. I was only in the house a minute, wasn't I?"

"Jump in my van and we will take a look around the block. He won't have gone far."

They circled the block a few times, with Pete stopping and Libby getting out to call. A few neighbours asked what the problem was and were horrified to know that cute pup they had seen her walking so often had gotten out of the yard. Everyone vowed to keep an eye out.

Pete parked the van at Libby's again. "I've still got some work to do to fix the leak. But I'll go look again when I am finished."

"Thanks for your help, Pete. That was kind of you." Libby could hardly speak she was so frozen with fear and disbelief.

"I'm going to go around on my bike and keep looking. Just close the door when you are all done, but leave the gate ajar in case Chance comes back. I never would have believed that he would just run off. Don't worry about the cats. They hop over the fence all the time but don't go far."

Adrenaline was racing through her body and she had to keep searching. The thought that something might happen

A New Leash on Life

to Chance terrified her. She rode her bike, trying to maintain control, all through the surrounding neighbourhoods.

Grudgingly she finally gave up, went in the house and burst into tears. She couldn't remember ever feeling so desperate. Her first reaction was to begin creating a poster on her computer to spread around town.

From her bike, she had called Marge and in between gulps and sputters told her what had happened.

Marge was in the middle of grocery shopping but came right over after checking out.

She gave Libby a long hug and Libby burst into tears again. "Sorry, I can't control myself!"

Marge handed her a tissue and led her to the sofa. "Of course you can't! Who could? Let's just sit for a moment and try to figure this out."

Chapter Fifteen

After collecting herself, Libby showed Marge she was already in the process of creating a poster on her computer and would print a pile of them. "As you can see, the print is large with a photo of Chance and really should get people's attention. I'm going to post them all over town. My phone number is there but I also said Chance is chipped and any vet can identify him. Fingers crossed!"

Marge held up her hand. "Wait! Wait! I called Patty on my way over. She's texting Deborah and Anne to get them to come here," Marge said, referring to their closest friends. "She said not to put your address or phone number on the poster."

"For heaven's sake, why not? That doesn't make any sense!"

"Well, Patty spoke very differently about that. Being a cop, she knows what she is talking about. She is going to bring you another phone and you need to put that number on the poster."

"Another phone? Really?"

A New Leash on Life

"She said she will talk to you about it when she gets here and explain in detail. But briefly she said there are too many weirdos out there."

Marge's phone rang. "Okay, we are on it," she said to Libby when she finished the call. "Patty, Deborah and Anne are on the way here to collect the posters and will put them up everywhere once you change the phone number. You've had enough to deal with today and they want to do this for you. But you can't print them until Patty sees them."

When the women arrived, Patty took charge after they all comforted Libby and expressed their horror at Chance's disappearance.

"Listen up, my friends. The reason I'm giving Libby this phone is to maintain her privacy. If she puts her phone number on the poster, I promise you she will begin to receive all sorts of crank calls. We want those calls on this burner phone."

Everyone's jaw dropped. "You are kidding," Anne exclaimed.

"Not one bit," Patty assured her. "For the same reason you must not put your home address on either."

"That's horrible," Libby said, with shock registering on her face.

"Sadly, our world has empowered all sorts of strange, sick people to get involved where they should not and cause chaos. Your privacy must be protected."

"But what if I miss a real call from an honest person?" Libby asked.

"When that happens, you will receive that call and recognize it for what it is. In the meantime, you can hang up on crank calls and erase them. Once Chance has been found, no one can keep calling you."

All three women expressed surprise at this situation but once they thought about it, believed Patty had a point.

"Thanks so much. I'm so grateful to you for doing this." Libby said, finding tears beginning to stream down her face again.

"Nonsense," Anne said. "You've had enough of a shock today and you don't need to be reminded every time you put up a poster and look at Chance's sweet face. It's the least we can do."

Marge suggested to Libby that they set up social media posts and call the police in the meantime.

"Well, how about coming back when you are through. There's sauvignon blanc chilling in the bar fridge and we will all be ready for a glass or two," Libby said to the poster team.

Two hours later, they all arrived back and reported how kind everyone had been when they saw the poster and heard the story.

"The whole town is on the lookout," Deborah declared. "We divided up. I took some to the vet clinics, the library, the marina, the dog park and all the supermarkets."

Patty added, "I went to Barks & Brews, Beachside Brews Coffee Shop, The Patty Shop, Dogtopia, the yoga studio, and all through downtown. This is such an amazing dog town, everyone is on alert."

Anne reported that she had seen a woman walking a pup that looked like Chance in the Blue Moon RV Park. "My heart leapt because I thought perhaps I had found him! It turned out to be a woman named Dorothy who had a pup from the same litter as yours. She was beside herself when I told her what happened and insisted on taking a bunch of posters. She said she would put them everywhere in the development. She hugged her dog, Sadie she called

A New Leash on Life

her, and said her heart would break if anything happened to her. What a sweetie."

"What a coincidence..." Libby murmured, her heart hurting even more.

Anne continued by saying she had also gone to the various parks and left posters at all the entrances.

"I didn't get a chance to stop and drop off posters at Beach Reads, but I will tomorrow first thing," Anne said. "Hopefully Chance will be back in no time after this and we won't need to."

"Wow, you gals are amazing. I cannot thank you enough," Libby said.

"I'm sure he will turn up," Marge said, attempting to be comforting. "I know it sounds cliché, but we have to keep hoping."

"Of course, that's all I can think about," Libby murmured, with a catch in her voice.

"Let me pour the wine. We all need to relax for a while," Marge said.

After her friends had left, Libby sat and thought how fortunate she was to have these wonderful women in her life. They had known each other for many years and it was at times like this that they all pulled together no matter what.

Sleep did not come easily that night.

The following morning, she wakened, unrested, and thinking of Chance before anything else. At first, she saw a vision of him running to her and she felt inspired. But within seconds that bubble burst. Then she saw him lying in a ditch or, just as terrible, in the hands of dognappers. She had read many times before how there were gangs of people who stole healthy dogs for which there was a market.

That could be it. The thought horrified her.

She googled 'dognapping in Florida' and was shocked to read that over two million dogs are stolen in America every year. It said half of all thefts are from the yard of their home, which made her feel even worse. The article also said that 93% of stolen dogs are recovered. So that gave her hope.

That afternoon Marge dropped by and Libby told her what she had read. "Can you believe it? Often the dognappers wait until a reward is posted and then bring the dog back claiming to have found it wandering."

"Sick people," Marge muttered.

"Maybe I should have put a reward on the poster I made. What do you think? It never even occurred to me that this might have happened."

"Well, don't beat yourself up about it. We are all too trusting and keep forgetting that the world is a different place than the one in which we grew up" Marge said. "Let's wait a while more and see if Chance is found. We can always post another flyer later with a reward."

Chapter Sixteen

The next morning Libby got on her bike at 6:30 a.m. The sun was just up but the air still cool. She rode slowly through a different part of town before the day became hot. She carried both phones with her but there were no calls about Chance, just sympathetic calls from friends saying they were watching for him.

Later, she dropped off posters at the police station. The officer on duty at the desk was compassionate and assured her they would be on the lookout. He also doublechecked that she had not put her real phone number on the poster.

"My friend is a police officer and she brought me a burner to use."

A handsome young officer with piercing blue eyes was standing nearby and commented, "That's exactly the right thing to do! What a good friend to have. Hi Mrs. Moore, I met you not long ago at Barks and Brews when I was waiting for Emily to finish work. I'm so sorry to hear that this is your pup."

"Oh right! Officer Fischer, nice to see you ... and thank you. I'm beside myself!"

"Call me Kuno. I know how you must feel. Try not to worry. Honestly, lost dogs usually are found. Keep believing. We will do everything we can to help."

His warm smile and calm manner gave her hope.

Libby thanked him as he walked outside with her to where she had left her bike. "I appreciate everything being done, Kuno. Thank you again for helping me feel a bit better."

A day later, a pleasant-sounding woman with a deep syrupy southern accent called on the burner phone.

"Honey, I believe I've found your sweet little poochie. He was wanderin' around my neighbourhood this morning and I brought him home to my place. He's so sweet and cuddly I'm tempted to keep him forever."

Libby tried to reply calmly. Patty had been very clear about what she should say to any stranger who called. "That is wonderful news! I'll be happy to come and pick him up right away or meet you at your local police station, if that is convenient."

"It's sure enough not convenient, dearie, but I'll bring him to your place. He's such a sweetie, I'm sure you are anxious to have him back in your lil' ol' arms."

"You are right about that. He's a cutie. I especially love the white tip on his tail." Patty had instructed her to add this incorrect information to the conversation.

"Ah looove that too! It's just adorable! Y'all must by cryin' your eyes out day and night. How much is the reward?"

Libby's heart broke. This proved the woman did not

A New Leash on Life

have Chance. To be certain, she suggested meeting again at the woman's house or the police station.

At this, the woman became very agitated. "Y'all will never see your stupid dog on God's green earth again, you crazy lady!" A stream of expletives followed before the caller slammed down the phone.

Libby was distraught, worried she had done the wrong thing. Maybe the woman did have Chance and was just confused about the white tip on his tail. She called Patty immediately who confirmed she had done the right thing. "That woman does not have Chance. She's a nutbar. I'm so sorry."

Every day Libby continued to ride her bike through different neighbourhoods early in the morning or in the cool of the evening before sunset.

And every day, her heart broke all over again. Especially when the predicted crank calls kept happening.

At times the calls were obviously from kids, thinking they were being smart. Some offered to return the dog for money.

"Do they really think someone would fall for that?" Libby wondered. But no matter how ridiculous the calls were, they hurt and were bothersome.

It was troubling to hear strangers' abusive language accusing her of not taking care of her pup. "Why weren't you watching him?" "How could you leave him on his own?" "You do not deserve to have a pet."

She couldn't stop wondering what these people were missing in their lives that caused them to spend time in such a senseless and hurtful pursuit.

She remembered when she was a child, she and some of her friends would make prank calls asking a stranger if their refrigerator was running. When the person said yes, they would say, "Well you better catch it before it runs away" and then hang up. They would laugh their heads off. But they were just kids being silly. These calls she was receiving were not silly. But maybe the people making these awful calls were laughing their heads off too. The world had changed.

The hours after sunset were the most difficult so Libby immersed herself in baking. All of her neighbours and friends were familiar with her culinary skills and she had already established the routine of creating a layered cake with velvety frosting and cupcakes for Serenity Palms once a week.

Each evening as she felt a curtain of gloom descending, she put on the well-worn, smocked apron that had belonged to her dear Gram and whipped up many of her favourite recipes.

The kitchen hummed with an electric energy, the air thick with the scent of vanilla, chocolate, and butter. It was a baking frenzy, a symphony of mixing bowls clinking, her oven and timers chiming,

Her beloved Gram was Canadian and whenever Libby baked her recipes of butter tarts or Nanaimo bars, people clamored for more. She added scrumptious date squares, rich brownies swirled with caramel, and tangy lemon bars dusted with powdered sugar, to the repertoire.

Other nights she whipped up batches of classic chocolate chip cookies, her hands a blur as she measured flour, cracked eggs, and folded in morsels of chocolate with precision. She had baked these for so many years for Matthew and then for her grandchildren, sweet memories filled the room along with the aroma of the warm, fresh baking. She chuckled remembering how she often surprised them with little changes to the recipe.

A New Leash on Life

When the last cookie trays and glass baking dishes were removed from the oven or placed in the refrigerator, Libby would step back to admire her handiwork and hope it all brought joy and delight to everyone who shared them. The good feeling barely began to compensate before sadness set in again.

Then she would fill her deep bathtub to the brim, add plenty of bath salts, and sink down to try to soak her sadness away.

She could not believe how profoundly she loved Chance in such a short time. Although she loved Max and Mimi, she now understood a dog's affection was entirely different. Those expressive dark eyes seemed to look directly into her soul and promise unconditional love.

The comfort, laughter and companionship filled the emptiness in her heart that had come with losing Don as her partner and her role as librarian. Libby realized she had not understood how much she needed everything this sweet pup so lovingly gave to her.

Libby knew about grief. She had suffered through it with the loss of her parents and more recently with the loss of dear friends. Even though Don was still alive there was definitely grief involved with watching his disease take over his life. Moving him to Serenity Palms had not been easy.

Living with the love Chance brought to each day, softened the pain.

She often thought of the words her pastor had shared with her after a Sunday service soon after Don had moved.

"Grief comes in many colors," her pastor said. He took her arm and walked with her to a bench in a quiet part of the manicured churchyard, behind the historic stone church.

"Everyone experiences it in different ways and for

different reasons. The most important thing to remember is that your journey is unique and you must allow yourself to grieve at your own pace. I am always here for comfort, Libby. Don't ever hesitate to ask."

Those thoughts and that conversation remained with Libby as the days went by.

She was reminded by them to reach out to Leo at Beach Reads. If anyone understood grief, it was her. She'd told Leo when she'd picked up her books that if there was anything she could do for her, but Leo had brushed her off—very politely. And Libby understood. Sometimes grief was so deep you had to wade into a shallower spot before you could even reach for an outstretched hand. Again, she wondered how Leo was managing with two pups and hoped they were cuddly little life buoys.

She drove by the bookstore and noticed the yellow French door entrance was open. With its bright orange exterior and turquoise shutters with cut outs of seashells, fish and turtles, the look of the shop always made Libby smile. It was heartbreaking to know the sadness it held after Vrai's passing.

A few customers were leaving as Libby entered. She hesitated at the thought of letting Leo know about Chance, there was no way she wanted to bring sadness to Leo's already injured heart. On the other hand, she knew that many people would go into the book store on a daily basis and someone might know something about Chance.

"Hi Leo, how is business? Are you beginning to get into

the swing of things? I know everyone is elated to have the store open again."

Leo gave her a gracious smile. "Hey Libby. It's lovely to see you. I've been meaning to call."

"No worries. I can only imagine how busy you are not only running the business but getting those two sweet pups of yours settled in. How's that going?"

"Thanks for asking. There seems to be some balance in my life now. The pups are definitely keeping me busy and filling my heart with joy. I'm able to think about Vrai without breaking down ... at least not every time now. How are you doing?"

Libby hesitated. She knew she had to share her news. "I'm so glad to hear you are feeling better about everything, Leo. It's amazing how these pups can help heal our pain. Chance has certainly helped me. But ... the bad news is that he has gone missing."

Leo's expression clouded. "How awful. What happened?"

Libby shared the details and showed her a poster. "I'm in shock but also am focussed on being hopeful. There has to be an explanation. Kuno was very reassuring and told me most dogs who go missing are found. I'm going to hang on to that."

Leo stepped forward and hugged Libby. "I'm so so sorry! How random is that! Leave me a handful of posters and I'll share them as well as put some up in here."

They chatted for a few minutes and made plans to spend an evening together soon.

As she drove away, Libby felt content that Leo appeared to be coping with her new world. She was relieved that she managed to keep her tears in check and not trigger the sadness she knew Leo would still be carrying in her heart.

Chapter Seventeen

As the days progressed with no word, Libby continued to try to focus at keeping herself busy after her early morning searches on her bike. Of course, there were her daily visits to Don which were helpful in one way but it was difficult to hide her sadness.

With her tennis group two mornings a week, yoga whenever she wanted to go, and visits to the library ... which became more and more extended that week ... she was thankful for the distractions.

She joined her regular hiking group on Friday and they drove a few miles out of town to a trail that followed an abandoned rail line. This was one park where she had planned to take Chance because of the shade it offered along the way.

As she walked, she thought about the fun that would be and promised herself it would happen. She could not stop believing that Chance would be back.

The walk was easy but long and once you committed to a certain stretch, it was necessary to see it through. The path alternated between well forested areas and swampy parts where binoculars came in handy to identify the many species of birds, and the odd alligator basking in the sun.

"I'm not giving up hope," she told her friends as the weekend loomed.

"No, you should not," they agreed, adding, "It's early days yet." Even when it didn't feel that way. She felt she was living in slow motion and that every day stretched on and on.

"Well," Libby continued, "I did think I would have heard something by now. I really did. So I'm trying not to feel pessimistic about it."

Her friends kept calling and dropping by. They made plans to keep her busy and hopefully distracted from what might be an exercise in futility, although no one wanted to admit it.

They all agreed they were enjoying her baking marathons and teased her about that.

All of the staff at Serenity Palms had joined in sharing posters at the residence and asking visitors if they had seen Chance wandering around. They offered words of hope every day and Libby was touched by their caring.

On the weekend, Libby and Marge went for a long walk on the beach just after sunrise. With their shoes off, the soft, warm sand caressed their feet and the sound of the waves was comforting with no loud voices to disturb the ambiance.

The town had a new project called Baskets for Beaches and at several points there were yellow baskets people could carry on their walk and place trash in as they went along. Then at other points there were trash bins where you could empty your basket and hang it up for someone else or carry it on further.

"Isn't it great to see how many people are getting involved in this?" Marge commented. "And I particularly love how many young people, even kids, are being part of it!"

Libby nodded, but her eyes were beginning to take on a haunted look. "The crank calls are really getting to me. I'm losing hope for humanity ... seriously. There have been so many. Thank goodness for Patty and the second phone."

Every time they came across a dog, Libby could not stop herself from pausing and talking to it. Which only made the situation worse.

By the end of the weekend, Libby was an anguished wreck. Lack of sleep and loss of appetite were taking their tolls. She cancelled a tennis game on the weekend and everyone was understanding.

Instead she sat by the pool in between swimming vigorous laps that left her breathless. Somehow, she had to rid herself of the intense pain and sadness. If Chance was gone for good there was nothing more she could do. It was time to pull herself together and move on. So far, her efforts were not working.

She tried not to show it but the disappearance had truly thrown her for a loop. She had not fully realized how much her emotions were tied up in the connection they had established in the short time Chance had been with her.

Thinking that Chance might be gone from her forever caused her to feel deep pain and loss. It was as though she had lost a child. She told herself that felt like an overly dramatic reaction but she could not shake it. The emotions were profound as she kept reliving memories of the time they had shared.

She couldn't stop herself from scrolling through the hundreds of photos she had taken since Chance came into her life five months before. Some made her laugh and others made her cry.

Her thoughts were constantly disrupted by terrible images of Chance lying injured or stuck or wandering somewhere. Had he really run off on his own? Had he been stolen? Was it her fault? Had she not closed the gate properly?

Even the cats appeared glum. They lay around in Chance's crates, seeming sad and listless. They were not interested in their playtimes or zoomies. They had always been affectionate but never more so than now. It was as if they sensed Libby was suffering.

Since Leslie was not around, Libby called Emily. She needed to talk to someone whose heart she knew was connected to her dog.

Emily tried to console Libby in their phone chat and help her feel hopeful, but Libby could tell from her voice that she was concerned.

"Kuno mentioned he spoke to you at the station the other day when you dropped off some posters," Emily said.

"Oh Emily, he was so kind and consoling ... and may I say, how good looking he is, which doesn't hurt!"

Emily chuckled. "I'm glad to see your sense of humor is still intact. I agree. He is a sweetie! He told me how everyone at the station was hoping to help find your pup."

"That's good to know. I cannot stop beating myself up and feeling guilty about Chance's disappearance."

"I understand. But you have to stop that. Just keep your hope alive and know the whole neighbourhood is trying to help."

A New Leash on Life

She avoided video calls from Australia and pretended she was not at home when she did answer the phone, saying Chance was not with her. She knew she would break into tears if she told them what had happened. But she also knew she was running out of time and would have to be honest about it soon.

Libby's phone rang on the morning of the eighth day. Each time it rang, Libby had to take a moment to compose herself and not let her hopes take over.

It was Doctor Sawyer.

Libby's gut tightened. She did not want to tell him what had happened.

"Hello Libby! I have good news for you. Chance is sitting here at my office! He is just fine and waiting for you to come and collect him. I'm sure this past week has been dreadful for you."

"Dreadful d-d-doesn't begin to cover it!" Libby sputtered, as she wept with relief and choked out the words, "I'm on my way."

Chapter Eighteen

Libby hoped she didn't pass a radar cop on the way to the clinic. She tried to keep her speed down but was more than slightly out of control. Blinded by tears and fuelled by adrenaline, she gripped the steering wheel with white-knuckled intensity, her foot pressed hard on the accelerator. She was thankful it was not far to go and called Marge on the way.

She burst through the door into the sterile reception area and threw her arms around Chance who was perched on a chair. He whimpered uncontrollably when he saw her and when she stepped back he leapt into her arms.

Libby swallowed hard and squeezed her eyes shut, struggling to regain her composure. To no avail. Her cheeks were covered with tears and no words were possible. Chance was back. Her heart was overflowing.

Doctor Sawyer was smiling broadly as Chance squirmed happily in Libby's arms, wriggling with excitement and licking her face in a frenzy.

Next to Doctor Sawyer was a frail-looking, white-haired lady with crutches. A full- length cast covered her left leg from thigh to ankle. Grasping the woman's hand was a curly-haired, freckle-faced little girl who appeared to be about six and reminded Libby of a young Shirley Temple. The little girl was in tears and sniffling loudly.

The woman began apologizing repeatedly. The little girl sobbed.

Doctor Sawyer patted the woman's hand and said, "There, there. Perhaps it would be best if I explained for you. Libby Moore, this is Matilda Brown and her granddaughter, Rosie."

The women nodded tentatively to each other in acknowledgement. Rosie looked at Chance and cried even louder.

Libby took a deep breath and pulled herself together as best she could.

Doctor Sawyer continued. "As I understand it, Rosie lives with Mrs. Brown because her daughter, Rosie's mother, is often working out of town. Last Monday, a week ago yesterday to be exact, Mrs. Brown's nephew, Richard, was supposed to be taking care of Rosie. Mrs. Brown was in the hospital after surgery on her leg. She had a terrible accident the week before when she fell down some stairs at a meeting of the ladies auxiliary at her church."

Mrs. Brown interrupted. Her voice was weak and trembling. "Richard is a good young man but doesn't always make the best decisions ... I'm so sorry, so, so, sorry ...!"

Doctor Sawyer held up his hand. "Please, Mrs. Brown, let me continue."

With a grateful expression, she nodded and silently twisted a tissue in her hands.

Doctor Sawyer cleared his throat and continued. "Richard had looked after Rosie on the weekend and was anxious to go somewhere with friends on Monday. He didn't want to leave Rosie alone but could not find anyone to stay with her. He was driving around when he happened to see Chance alone in your yard, right by the gate. Without thinking, and seeing no one around, he hopped out of his car, grabbed Chance ... who apparently was very friendly ... and drove off. He told Rosie the dog would keep her company."

"She ... she ... she did keep me company and made me laugh. She cuddled with me and I wasn't afraid when she was with me ..." Rosie blurted in between sobs, never taking her eyes off Chance.

Libby was listening carefully, putting all the details together.

"I'm so ashamed of my nephew," Matilda said. "First of all, he should never have left Rosie alone, period! Not even with a dog! And certainly not a dog he had stolen! I just came home from the hospital this morning to discover what had happened. Rosie begged me not to take the dog away. After I explained what Richard had done, she understood ... sort of ... but still wants to keep the dog."

She dabbed at her eyes with a tissue and sighed in exasperation.

Doctor Sawyer continued. "Mrs. Brown saw your poster and read that most dogs are chipped these days. She came here in a taxi immediately."

"I saw that paper with the dog's photo on a lamp post right beside our driveway, when I was brought home. I nearly fainted when I walked in and saw that same dog on the couch with Rosie." Mrs. Brown explained.

Her voice was filled with worry and apprehension. "I hope you won't report Richard to the police. It's just that he's been unemployed for a while and he and his friends had a chance for a job. He was kind of desperate."

A New Leash on Life

Chance was now nestled on Libby's lap, with Rosie's eyes still glued on him.

Libby was thinking the whole situation through as the story unfolded. Finally, she found her voice. "Do you mean your granddaughter was alone with Chance every day this week?"

Mrs. Brown nodded, her eyes downcast. Her lips were tight as her quiet voice betrayed sadness and outrage. "I didn't realize it. I thought Richard was with her but he went out on this job every day."

Rosie looked at the floor for moment, as if she felt the tension in the room.

Libby felt a surge of anger that the vulnerable little girl had been left alone.

Doctor Sawyer shook his head. "It was a case of Richard making some very unwise decisions and Rosie being a very brave little girl."

Rosie suddenly spoke with a torrent of words. "I was only brave because of Goldie. That's what I called the dog. I didn't know it was a boy. Uncle Richie brought dog food and a leash and told me I had to take Goldie out in the back yard to go to the bathroom. So I did. And she slept in bed with me every night."

She sniffed loudly and wiped her nose with the back of her hand. Tears streamed down her cheeks. As if she needed to protect her uncle she added, "Uncle Richie left me a phone to call him if I was scared. But I never was. He brought me chicken fingers every night. They're my favorite. Goldie likes them too."

Libby was so happy to have Chance back, she didn't even flinch at the thought of him eating Chicken Fingers for a week.

Rosie took a deep breath and finished by saying, "Uncle Richie didn't mean to be bad."

Mrs. Brown handed Rosie a crumpled tissue from her pocket.

"Thank you, Mrs. Brown ... and Rosie," Libby began, after a long pause.

"Please call me Matilda," Mrs. Brown interrupted.

"Thank you, Matilda," Libby began again. "I'm so sorry to see your injury. It was good of you to come straight over with Chance. Rosie, thank you for bringing Chance here and taking such good care of him this week. You can imagine how worried I was."

Mrs. Brown nodded, nervously twisting the tissue even harder. Rosie looked at Libby with hooded eyes and more of a scowl.

"I'm certainly not going to call the police, even though what Richard did was very wrong and irresponsible. But I also understand how the opportunity of a job must have been extremely important to him. The primary issue is that everything has ended well. Rosie is fine. Chance is here and has not suffered."

"Can I come to visit her?" Rosie asked. "I love her ... I mean him ... so so much even though he isn't a girl."

Mrs. Brown hushed her and shook her head. "Rosie!"

Libby smiled. "Of course you may. I'm sure Chance would love to have you visit and play with him. Would you like to give him a hug now?"

Rosie threw her arms around Chance, who covered her face with licks.

Mrs. Brown shook her head in embarrassment, fidgeting in her chair. "No ... really ... that is not necessary."

Libby patted the grandmother's arm. "I can imagine how Chance and Rosie became good friends spending all that time together. Tell me where you live and I will see how we can make a visit work. In fact, why don't Chance and I drive you home? Then I will see for myself."

Again, Mrs. Brown began to protest, but Doctor Sawyer intervened before she could say anything more.

Doctor Sawyer stood. "I think that sounds like a lovely idea, Libby. Thank you for being so understanding. I can assure you Chance has not suffered. He's in great shape and I want to congratulate you again on how well behaved he is. He's quite extraordinary."

Libby grinned, immense relief evident in her eyes. "Thanks so much. I couldn't agree more. He's a special boy. What a load off my mind this is. And no worries, case closed."

Doctor Sawyer turned to Mrs. Brown, shook her hand and then shook Rosie's hand. "Thank you for bringing Chance here. That was the right thing to do."

Chapter Nineteen

With Matilda giving directions, Libby soon pulled up her car in a neighbourhood ten minutes from her own. The small modular homes were in an older development that backed onto a public park with swings and baseball diamonds.

Many of the homes looked tired and the yards appeared neglected, but the one they stopped at had a tidy lawn and a garden filled with colorful hibiscus in full bloom and obviously well-tended.

"I've lived here for more than fifty years," Matilda said. "And I'm going to be 80 next month, so that's a lot of memories. These places were all new when we moved in."

"Lots of history here, for sure," Libby agreed. "I can see that you love to garden."

"Well, I don't know how much gardening I will ever be able to do again after this injury. I'll just have to wait and see."

"I will help you, Granny!" Rosie offered, her voice filled with affection.

"I know you will, my sweet girl. You love to work in the

A New Leash on Life

garden as much as I do," Matilda replied, her eyes glistening.

Libby got out and opened the doors for her passengers. Rosie gave Chance another hug. "I hope I will see you soon, Goldie ... I mean, Chance ... what kind of name is that anyway? I like Goldie way better."

Matilda looked grim and shook her head. Libby laughed. She thought Rosie was one of the most delightful little girls she had met in a long time.

"I will tell you about his name one day. And yes, you will see Chance soon," Libby said to her. "Your grandmother and I will arrange something."

She offered a hand to Matilda, who leaned in to whisper in her ear. "Thank you for being so gracious and understanding, dear. You didn't need to be."

Libby looked into Matilda's kindly eyes. "It is easy to recognize good people. I would like to have you and Rosie over for lunch whenever you are ready. In the meantime, tell me a good day to pick up Rosie to come and visit with Chance. She can spend the day if she likes. We can play it by ear."

She handed Matilda a card with her contact information. "Let's have her come soon. And if you need some help with things while your leg is in a cast, just call me. I'm not far away."

As she drove home, Libby thought about the serendipity some unexpected incidents bring into people's lives. She had a feeling that Matilda and Rosie were about to become part of hers.

Libby laughed as Chance pushed past her into the house. He seemed as happy to be home as she was to have him back.

Max and Mimi leapt from their perch on the windowsill to greet him. A serious case of zoomies ensued as Libby felt an overwhelming sense of wellbeing. After a week of shock and worry ... and loss ... everything felt harmonious and she was in sync with it. She had a deep moment of clarity that this was how home should feel.

And just as that thought finished, she realized she needed to call Leo at Beach Reads right away. Her other friends would find out about Chance's safe return soon enough if they hadn't heard it from Marge already.

Leo answered on the first ring and Libby babbled her good news. To her dismay, Leo broke into noisy tears.

There was an awkward silence, as Libby tried to figure out what to say.

"I'm sorry," Leo exclaimed, saving Libby from having to speak. "It's just I'm so happy, so unbelievably, crazily happy for you. Thank you. *Thank you.*"

It was kind of a strange exchange, but Libby thought she understood what Leo meant. Sometimes people hesitated to share good news or happy life events with people who were grieving, thinking it might be salt in the wound. And perhaps for some it was, but for others, hearing good news or happy resolutions to some of life's hard events, was immensely comforting.

She felt happy she had made the call.

Chapter Twenty

Everyone at Serenity Palms was immensely relieved to see Libby arrive with Chance the next afternoon. The residents waiting to greet Chance in the hall were more animated than usual as they welcomed him all the way down the long corridor.

While they were alone, Libby told the entire story to Don who did not respond in any way. Somehow despite that, it made her feel better to share it with him.

Her heart lifted as Don's hand moved to Chance's back and he began stroking it the minute Libby sat him on his lap.

She vaguely wondered how much longer Chance would fit there at the rate he was growing and Don was shrinking. He weighed almost 35 pounds when he was at the groomer's that morning. Libby had noticed that he had not been brushed the previous week and the groomer went out of her way to fit him in. Like everyone, she had been terribly worried while he was missing.

Dorothy helped Don into a wheelchair and Libby took over once they were outside.

"Enjoy your walk and just buzz me if you need to," Dorothy said. She gave Chance a pat on his head. "We are all so relieved Chance is home safe and sound."

Libby attached the leash to a special belt she had purchased. It left her hands free to push the wheelchair and help Don with anything he might need.

She chose the more shaded pathways and stopped at a bench by the side of a pond. A fountain in the middle had three levels of water gently cascading. Don soon fell fast asleep and so did Chance.

Libby took out her phone and read a few chapters of a thriller she was enjoying. After the fear and worry of the previous week, she relished the calm atmosphere and was filled with gratitude that everything had worked out.

In the evening, Libby's phone rang.

"Hello Mrs. Moore, it's Matilda Brown."

"Matilda, it's lovely to hear from you but before you go any further, if you want me to call you Matilda, then you must call me Libby. It's only fair."

There was a moment of hesitation before Matilda replied, "Okay Libby. Thank you. I will do that. I wanted to speak to you about Rosie so you would understand the situation here a little better."

"As you wish," Libby said. "But please do not feel it is necessary to explain anything."

Matilda continued. "Rosie's mother is a dancer in Las Vegas. Every once in a while, she gets a job at the casinos around here. But Vegas is where the big money is for her. So

Rosie has lived with me most of her life. My little Rosebud. I love her with all my heart."

"I'm certain you do, Matilda. Even in the few moments I was in her company I could tell she is delightful and kind. I could also see how you are devoted to each other."

Matilda continued. "Rosie can't wait to go to school in September and is excited to go into grade one. She missed going to kindergarten at Dragonfly Cove last year because her mother took her to Vegas to live with her. It turned out to be a disaster and thank goodness the social services sent her back to live with me. The only good thing that came out of it was that Rosie taught herself to read. She was stuck in front of a television every day and thankfully figured out how to find channels that taught her about learning."

"Hmmm, I wondered why I had not seen her at my school last year. That explains it. I was the librarian and know that there was not one child I did not get to know."

Matilda was not finished. "One other thing you should know. Rosie rarely speaks. Seldom to anyone but her mother and me. Not even to Richard. But apparently when your dog was here, she talked to him constantly. I saw that as soon as I got home and Richard told me last night that every night she would sit in the back yard or in her room and talk to ... Goldie ... as she called her ... er, him. It was quite remarkable."

"That is very sweet. It's wonderful you have discovered how Rosie related to Chance and how that has helped her. I retired from my job last December but was at the public school for forty years. I absolutely loved working with children and will be happy to assist Rosie with anything at all."

"Thank you, that is so kind, ... and thank you for your invitation to lunch. If you don't mind, I would like to wait until I no longer need crutches, but Rosie would love to visit with you and Chance."

"I understand completely. It's awkward getting around on crutches. When would you like Rosie to come over? I will pick her up."

Matilda hesitated. Libby repeated her question, adding, "No need to be shy about it."

"Well, um, Rosie has not stopped asking me since we got home yesterday."

"Great," Libby replied. "How does this sound? I will be playing tennis tomorrow morning and Chance will be with me. We will stop on our way home and collect Rosie around 10:30. We start playing at 8 a.m. to avoid the heat. Please have her bring a bathing suit, if she wishes, as I have a pool."

"Oh goodness gracious me!" Matilda declared. "She will be busting with joy when I tell her. No sleep for her tonight!"

Libby laughed. "Fine then, Matilda, I will see you tomorrow morning at 10:30. I'm already looking forward to it and so will Chance when I tell him."

Matilda laughed. "That's so funny! See you tomorrow!"

Chapter Twenty-One

When Libby pulled into the driveway at Matilda's, Rosie was sitting in a red canvas fold-up chair at the entrance to the carport. Libby grinned as the little girl's face lit up when she leapt to her feet. Her strawberry blond curls bounced and glistened in the sun, adding to the picture of innocence and exuberance.

She grabbed a small paper bag that was beside her chair, as Libby got out of the car.

When he saw Rosie, Chance wiggled playfully in the back seat, despite being restrained by his car harness.

Rosie shyly said hello to Libby. She climbed into the back seat with Chance when Libby asked if she would like to sit there, and immediately threw her arms around him as he covered her with his puppy kisses.

Matilda came out the side door of the house and quietly greeted Libby. "Thank you again for taking Rosie. She has been sitting out here since she got up, even though I had given her a clock so she could see when you would be here.

My goodness she has a mind of her own. You bring her back when you have had enough."

Libby laughed and shook her head. "I'm sure we will have a lovely day. I will bring her back around mid-afternoon. That is when I will go to visit my husband at Serenity Palms."

"I understand," Matilda said. "Rosebud has her lunch in her bag, so she won't be any additional work for you. I added a few extra cookies for you."

Libby smiled warmly. "That's very thoughtful. Don't worry about us. And please call me if you want to check on Rosie. I have to make a quick stop at the library and then we will be at home after that."

Matilda took Libby's arm and moved her a bit away from the car before speaking in almost a whisper. "As I explained to you, Rosie has been exposed to some traumatic situations in her young life. If you feel she seems to be anxious, please bring her home."

Libby felt a wrench in her heart for this sweet woman whose love for Rosie was clear. "Please do not worry. I will watch her carefully and be sure to let you know if we need to come back."

Libby got in the car. Rosie gave Matilda a hug through the open back window, saying "I love you, Granny. Don't worry."

As they waved goodbye, Rosie had already begun a nonstop chat with Chance. Libby smiled.

After they left the driveway, Libby turned to the youngster.

"Rosie, I have to drive by the bin at the side of the library and drop in the books I am returning."

Rosie said nothing for a moment and Libby contem-

A New Leash on Life

plated what Matilda had said concerning her not speaking to others.

Then in a quiet voice, words began tumbling out. "What do you mean? I've never been to a library. What's the bin? Is it far?"

"Well, nothing is really far in this small town and the bin is where you can simply drop off the books you have read," Libby said. And then she had an idea. "Do you know that you can borrow books at the library and take them home to look at or read and then return them?"

Silence again. Libby was about to say something else, when Rosie asked in almost a whisper.

"What kind of books?"

"Whatever kind you like. There are story books, chapter books, picture books, about every subject you can think of."

Rosie was wide-eyed and spoke a little louder. "For free?"

Libby grinned. But her heart sank to think Rosie had never been to a library.

"Would you like to come in with me and take a look? I will pick up a new book or two to take home."

Rosie hesitated. "But what about Chance? We can't leave him."

"You are right," Libby said. "But dogs are welcome in our library too. There is a small side yard where Chance can wait for us."

"Does it have a big fence?" Rosie asked with some alarm in her voice.

"It certainly does. Chance will be safe there. It has water bowls too. There is a shady place to rest if he gets tired of running around if other dogs are there."

Shyly, Rosie said, "Well ... yes... I would like to go in with you." Libby sensed the child's confidence growing.

"Could I look at books? I have some books we got at the church bazaar and I love them."

"Of course," Libby said. "If you like, we will get you your own library card and then you can visit the library any time and take out books. Your grandma might like to come with you when her leg is better."

"Granny can't read cuz her eyes are poorly, but we listen to music together. And what's a library card anyway?""

"Well, that's a very nice thing to do, listening to music with your grandmother," Libby said, making a note to ask about Matilda's vision and perhaps mention audiobooks to her. Then she explained to Rosie how the library works and what Rosie's card would be for.

Inside, Rosie followed Libby to a door off the foyer. Opening it, Chance joined a corgi and a cocker spaniel in a side yard. Tails wagging, they gave each other the once over before tumbling around in the small space.

Rosie stared at them. "Dogs can have fun here too. I like that!"

"You're absolutely right," Libby agreed.

Libby returned her books, picked up the new ones she had reserved, and organized a card for Rosie. As they went inside to the children's book section, Rosie's eyes sparkled.

"Wow! All these books are free?"

"Yes. Free to borrow. Isn't that great? As I said, there are books about everything you can imagine. So take your time and look around."

Libby showed Rosie where to find books about different subjects and then sat at a table. "I already picked up two new books as we walked by a shelf where they were on hold for me, so I will wait for you here. You can take your time

A New Leash on Life

and choose which books you would like to take home. Let me know if you want some help."

"Can I choose more than one?"

"You certainly can. I would suggest you start with three books and when you finish them we will return them and you can choose new ones."

Rosie stared at her in disbelief. Her mouth dropped open and she blinked rapidly, "You mean I can just take them? I don't have to pay anything?"

"That's correct, my dear. Isn't it wonderful? Of course, you need to take very good care of them. You can let me know when you are ready to change them and I will bring you back here so your grandmother doesn't need to worry about it. When you get bigger, you can ride your bike here."

"I don't have a bike," Rosie said. "But I like to walk."

"Well, perhaps when you are a bit older you will have one," Libby said. She thought about the collection of old bikes in Matthew's garage and planned to ask him if there was one that might be good for Rosie.

After a while, Rosie returned with a large pile of books. "Can I sit here for a while to choose which three I will borrow?"

"Absolutely. That's another of the nice things about the library. You can look at whatever books you like while you are here and when you are ready to choose, just put the other ones on a shelf on that cart over there. Someone who works here will put them away for you."

Rosie grinned with so much joy her face glowed. She pulled up a chair and began inspecting the books as Libby looked on.

Libby smiled, happy to see Rosie's response to the library. Introducing children to the joy of books and reading had been her life's work.

Chapter Twenty-Two

Rosie's day at Libby's was most enjoyable for all of them. Chance was happy to have two people to play with and cuddle. The cats appeared to like Rosie, following her from place to place, and she was excited to discover they lived at Libby's too.

"I really like cats. There are some that come to our yard sometimes and let me pet them. But mostly they run away."

Rosie was respectful and not nosy, as many young children might have been. While she played with Chance in the yard, Libby weeded the flower beds. She asked Rosie if she would like to pick a bouquet to take to her grandmother and watched with pleasure as she carefully made her choices.

Rosie insisted she would eat the peanut butter and jam sandwich she had brought along for her lunch. Libby made herself one as well and they sat at the dining table, overlooking the pool area.

"Rosie, would you like to look at your library books for a while after lunch? Then we can go in the pool to cool off."

"Oh yes, please! I can't wait to look at those books."

A New Leash on Life

Rosie looked nervously at the pool. "I don't know how to swim though so I will just sit on the steps. That would be fun."

"I still have all sorts of swim vests from when my grandchildren were young. I keep them for visits from friends with their grandchildren. I'm sure one of them will fit you."

"You're a grandma like my Granny?" Rosie asked in surprise. "You don't look like a grandma."

Libby chuckled. "Grandmas come in all sizes, shapes, and colors." Then she told Rosie about her family and how Chance was supposed to be theirs until they decided to stay in Australia.

"Wow. I guess you miss them but I'm glad they had to stay longer in that place. I might not have met Goldie …er… Chance. Where is that anyway? How do you get to see them?"

Libby brought out a book about Australia that she had purchased on her visit and they spent the next little while looking at pictures … mostly of koala bears. Rosie was full of curiosity and questions were non-stop.

When they went out to the lanai, Rosie looked quizzically at the mesh enclosures but said nothing.

"This is where I raise Monarch butterflies." Libby said, stopping in front of one.

"The orange ones?" Rosie asked.

"That's right. My husband started doing this years ago and I am doing it now that he cannot."

She pointed out some eggs, some bright green, white and black caterpillars and some pupae. A few butterflies were almost ready to emerge.

Rosie's jaw dropped as she began to understand what Libby was describing. "That's just like The Hungry Caterpillar! It's one of my favorite books."

Libby chuckled. "That's it exactly." Rosie had several questions before they went over to the lounges by the pool. "I think that having baby butterflies is a very nice thing to do and I hope I get to help you let them fly away when it is time."

"I'll be happy to have your help, my dear." She felt a brush of sadness, thinking how Don would have loved Rosie's reaction to it all.

Max and Mimi wandered around the pool patio and, at one point, Mimi hopped up on Rosie's lounge chair, to her delight.

"I love to hear that loud purring! I wish dogs purred too."

Libby grinned. "Wouldn't that be cool."

Later, wearing a swim vest over her bathing suit, Rosie cautiously went down the steps. Libby stayed beside her until she seemed to feel comfortable. Then she showed her how she could float on her back or just hold onto a foam floatie and bob around the pool. When the smile never left Rosie's face, Libby figured this was another happy experience for her.

After a while, Chance let them know he was awake from his nap in the crate. Rosie waited on the patio while Libby brought him into the pool. Then to great squeals from Rosie and lots of splashing from Chance, the three of them spent time together in the water.

Around 4 p.m. Libby explained to Rosie that it was time for her to visit her husband and she would take Rosie home on the way. There was another flood of questions as Rosie tried to understand why Libby's husband did not live with her now.

Having Chance home brought untold joy back to Libby and the presence of Rosie only added to that.

A New Leash on Life

"Here's your little Rosebud, Matilda. We had a lovely day and thank you for your delicious oatmeal cookies. I am taking two of them to my husband now."

Matilda beamed as Rosie gave her an enthusiastic hug. "We had so much fun!"

Then Rosie turned to Libby, shuffling her feet shyly. "Thank you, Mrs. M." She had asked Libby if it was all right to call her that after she heard two young previous students call Libby that at the library. "Is it okay if I give you a hug too?'

"I would like that very much, Rosie. It was great fun having you spend the day with us and we will do it again soon."

Rosie also gave Chance a hug plus a kiss on the top of his head.

"I'm not calling him Goldie any more, Granny," she said to Matilda. "After all, he is a boy. And now I know two cats and one is a girl!"

She collected her library books and Libby explained to Matilda why she had them, as she handed her the library card for safe keeping.

The lines around Matilda's eyes crinkled into a smile. "My goodness, Rosebud, I do believe you have had a very special day."

Rosie replied, nodding her head and grinning from ear to ear. "Yes, I did! And Mrs. M says I can go over every week to visit her and Chance. And the cats too! Can I? Is it okay?"

Libby was nodding her head before Matilda could ask her questions. "At least that. We had a lovely time and it was my pleasure ... and Chance's ... and the cats ... to spend the afternoon together. Let me know which day would be good next week. No hurry."

Matilda's eyes glistened. "I can't thank you enough." She leaned over and gently hugged Libby. "You truly are an angel."

On the drive over to Don's, Libby could not stop thinking how strangers can become friends under the most unexpected circumstances.

Chapter Twenty-Three

After a few weeks, Libby realized Rosie was becoming a part of her family in a comfortable, organic way. Libby enjoyed her company every Tuesday and sometimes more often. They also had begun reading a chapter book together. Rosie's enthusiasm for reading brought back happy memories of Libby's years in the library.

Rosie was thrilled to play with Chance and she also quickly became fond of the cats who were very affectionate with her.

"I love Chance the most," Rosie said one day. "But I love Max and Mimi too, especially because they purr. I love that special sound. It's kind of like they are humming me a song that they are happy."

Rosie had quickly lost her hesitation to chat and every day she visited Libby was filled with conversation that lifted Libby's heart. She was a naturally curious little girl with an innate kindness. It was as if Rosie had been storing up thoughts and feelings for much of her young life and was happy to finally feel she could set them free.

Rosie was introduced to Matthew, Amy, Kate and Jack in video chats and they were delighted to know this precocious, sweet little girl was keeping Libby and Chance good company.

Sitting around with Patty, Anne and Deborah late one afternoon after a spirited doubles match, the ladies had stopped in at Barks and Brews as they did once a month. Marge soon joined them when her match was over.

They were at their usual table, under a red and white striped umbrella. A light breeze was keeping the temperature comfortable and the ladies were feeling relaxed.

Without needing to order, Emily arrived with five gin and tonics on a tray and a small bowl of freshly sliced lime.

"Cheers, my friends and my Lab-owning sistah! Good to see you as always. I can't stop thinking of the torment you experienced. I would be an absolute wreck if it happened to me."

Libby gave her a comforting look. "But something really good came out of that terrible experience. You just never know what's going to happen in life."

She explained briefly about her new extended family and they all chatted with Emily for a few minutes before she excused herself. "That is so wonderful! Hey, the drinks are on me! No arguing! Now I better get back to work. Happy Hour, you know! Catch y'all later!"

They had recently celebrated Anne's birthday and now the conversation turned to the changes in life that several of them were facing. They had all known each other for decades and shared many memories. Through good times and difficult ones, they had celebrated together and lifted each other up without hesitation.

"A toast to friendship!" Anne said as she raised her glass. "Where would we be without it?"

"Got that right!" Deborah exclaimed. "You carried me through the worst years of my mother's illness and my father's horrible experience after Mom passed."

"Yikes! Don't remind me!" Patty said, rolling her eyes. "I mean, I'm sorry. I still feel sad about your Mom's struggles, but don't mention it in the same breath as your dad. He was something else."

"Yeah, I'm sorry. They definitely are two separate stories and my Mom loved all of you very much."

"Thank goodness, she was not ill for very long," Anne said.

"And she had such an amazing attitude about dying. I learned a lot from her," Libby said, as they all nodded in agreement.

Marge's eyes glistened. "She gave us all a good lesson in dying with dignity and making your own choices about that."

They all raised their glasses.

"But Patty", Deborah continued, "We learned something from my father's bad behaviour, you must admit. And we would not have sorted out that whole salacious situation without you being in the police force and having access to all that information. The four of you were my rocks."

Patty shook her head as she covered her face with her hands. She quickly regained her composure and said, "Let's face it, it really was your cockapoo who saved the day, Deb. He discovered that young woman hiding in your father's closet."

"You are right. Herbie was the hero of the day,"

Deborah said, with a wry grin, referring to her eight-year-old pet. "Even after all these years, we will never forget that whole mess! But it never would have been resolved without the police following up and getting my dad out of the grips of those scammers."

Anne nodded. "It really was a sad situation. And he was not the only senior to have that experience. I hope all the publicity helped other families be aware of some of the criminals out there preying on vulnerable older people. Thank goodness the police were right on top of it."

Patty nodded. "Those situations have become even more prevalent these days. At least your dad lived out his days peacefully at your brother's in New York."

"We've got to be on top of things, my friends, and have each other's backs," Marge said to a chorus of agreement.

Libby blew out a long sigh. "Well, here's a toast to Herbie! Another reason we love our pets!"

At the mention of his name, Herbie popped up his curly head from under the table where he was lying quietly with Chance and Patty's German shepherd, Ranger. All three dogs got up, as if they knew they were being talked about.

Within a minute, Emily was back with dog treats. "Happy Hour for the pups too!"

Chapter Twenty-Four

Autumn was a quiet time weather-wise to everyone's relief. The hurricane season did not amount to anything much in Dragonfly Cove. The hot humid days slowly transitioned into pleasant temperatures for hiking and Libby went out regularly.

Chance was a willing companion. As soon as Libby mentioned "walk" or "hike" to him, he would pull his leash off a hook by the side door and bring it to her, bouncing with energy.

He was growing into a good-sized teenaged Lab who loved to romp and wrestle. Libby felt she had never been in as good shape as she was since Chance grew out of his puppy phase. It quickly became apparent that she had to put energy into their playtimes and a sedate walk was not everything he needed.

Rosie loved to give him a good run around the yard when she visited and was not too girlie to roll around the grass with him. Her shrieks of delight filled the air.

The library visits were a treasured part of Rosie's time

with Libby, who introduced her to W. Bruce Cameron's wonderful dog stories which Rosie eagerly discussed with her.

As a librarian, Libby was familiar with Cameron's many series as she watched children of all ages devour them. She chuckled to herself now as she recalled they were not of any particular interest to her in those days. Now she was loving the books too.

Matilda was interested in Libby's suggestion of listening to audiobooks. Rosie often chose the same stories for Matilda so they could listen together and Matilda joined the library so she could order other audiobooks to be delivered to her.

Visits to the puppy park were a must so Chance could race around with whatever dogs happened to be there. One thing Libby had learned was how sociable dogs were and not discriminating at all. Breed, size, even age, were not factors. If the dog would run and play, that was all that mattered.

It amused her how often the smallest dogs would be leading the pack. Chance did not seem to feel he needed to be the boss; he was just there for the fun.

Libby also discovered that she was terrible at throwing a ball. She noticed others at the park with a long-handled ball holder that allowed the ball to soar through the air. She quickly acquired one to stop her embarrassment at throwing a ball that might go five feet sideways.

She enrolled Chance in one of Hank's obedience classes and he allowed Rosie to attend as well. Libby wanted to know that Chance would be obedient to her and Rosie was a willing and serious student.

Rosie's biggest issue was her fascination with Hank's many tattoos and his bizarre choices of clothing. From the beginning, Libby had a good conversation with Rosie about why she should not stare or giggle when she looked at him, whether he was wearing a leopard-spotted jogging suit or a black one-piece spandex body suit. The man had a magical way with helping dogs and humans interact, Libby explained, and that was what was important.

It was great fun spending time at classes with Allie and Marsha, who also had pups from the same litter as Chance.

As December approached, Libby's excitement grew. She was going to meet Matthew and his family in Hawaii for a two-week holiday over Christmas. They decided it was a perfect halfway point and would not put Libby through the long flight to Australia.

"Besides, it will be a lovely break for all of us", Libby said. She spoke with Doctor Sawyer about taking Chance on a plane and he assured her that he should be fine.

"He's strong and healthy and certainly never exhibits any signs of stress. I wish I were as relaxed as he is," he ended with a chuckle.

Rosie was sad Chance would not be with her at Christmas. "We bought a Santa hat at the Dollar Store for him to wear."

"Not to worry, Rosie. He will have a chance to do that." The little girl's eyes flashed with delight as Libby said, "We will have an early Christmas at my house."

Earlier in the month, Libby had asked Matilda if it would be acceptable for Rosie to give her a list of five items she might like. She was touched at the simplicity.

One bookmark.

One pad of drawing paper.
One box of ten pencil crayons
One bag of dog treats.
One sparkly hair band.

Rosie helped make Libby's grandmother's shortbread cookies on one of her visits. She and Libby sang along to Christmas music and Libby was happy to be reminded of similar memories with her children and grandchildren. Now Rosie was carrying on the tradition.

With her cheeks full of shortbread, Rosie declared the cookies to be the best she had ever tasted. Libby laughed with deep affection since that was what her entire family and all of their friends said year after year. It was such a simple recipe that everyone loved.

Ten days before Christmas, Rosie and Matilda came to Libby's for a festive celebration. Rosie was thrilled to bring the Santa hat for Chance to wear. "I've seen pictures of dogs at Christmas wearing a hat like this and now we have our own!"

Libby's heart filled whenever Rosie spoke about this new family circle of theirs as her own. She could feel the happiness they brought to each other and recognized how much it meant to her as well as Rosie and Matilda.

Matilda took a deep breath after coming into the house, which was filled with the aroma of roasting turkey. "Oh my! It has been a while since those unique smells wafted through my house. How wonderful."

She handed a ribbon bedecked jar of honey-glazed pecans to Libby saying "Richard sent these especially for you and here is a card for you to say thanks for being so good to us. He didn't seal it so I peeked at it." He had moved to North Carolina, with a full-time job, and sent money each month to Matilda.

"And Uncle Richie is sending me a bike for Christmas! I can ride to your place as soon as I learn not to fall off. His friend Bob is going to come over and teach me."

"That is wonderful!" Libby exclaimed. "We will be able to go for bike rides together."

Libby had prepared a full turkey dinner with stuffing, cranberry sauce and gravy.

Mashed potatoes were requested by Rosie and Libby invited her to the house the day before so she could help make that dish.

Matilda brought her special roasted carrots to pop in the oven along with the classic green bean recipe with crunchy onions.

"Those beans are my favorite ... except for Thanksgiving when I help make the sweet potato dish." Rosie burbled before slyly adding "It's really the marshmallows on top that I love the most."

Another of Libby's Christmas traditions was to prepare her own mincemeat tarts, Don's favorite. She had a tin of those ready to serve at home and another to take to Serenity Palms.

"Mmmm, yummy! But where is the meat?" Rosie had asked when she first tasted one.

Chance was busy chewing on his Christmas bone and Max and Mimi rolled around with their new catnip toys. The house was filled with Christmas joy.

Libby had the five gifts Rosie asked for plus one extra 'from Chance'. She also bought her a wooden easel on which to organize her drawing materials. It happened to come equipped with a full set of markers, crayons, pencils and paints.

Rosie had shown a talent for drawing and liked to create illustrations about the books she was reading. Libby was only too happy to encourage her. Rosie's gift to Libby was a sweet pencil sketch of Chance, colored with pencil crayons.

With a six-year-old's innocence of strokes, Chance was drawn in the middle of the page, with triangular ears on a round head featuring very expressive eyes. His long tail had short pencil strokes near it to indicate his tail was wagging. "Because it mostly always is," as Rosie explained.

The head and paws were a bit exaggerated adding to the endearing quality of the drawing. Libby could feel the love and effort in the heartwarming portrayal and could not stop smiling.

"Granny bought the special frame for it. I hope you like it."

"I love it. I can see you worked very hard on this portrait and it looks just like him. I will treasure it forever and we will keep it right here where everyone who comes to the house can see it." She kissed Rosie lightly on the cheek and Rosie gave her a long hug, whispering "I love you and Chance and Max and Mimi."

"We love you too, my sweet girl." Libby replied, feeling her heart ready to burst.

Matilda brought a large tin of her special Christmas cake which Libby declared "outstanding". She swooned over the moist and delicately balanced slices and Matilda coyly suggested it was the rum she used to soak the fruit for twenty-four hours.

Rosie said, "I'm not allowed to have it because the spirits will haunt me. It sounds like it should be something for Halloween, not Christmas."

A New Leash on Life

For Matilda, Libby had purchased a stunning pink Christmas cactus in full bloom with a gift card tucked discreetly into it for more plants from her favorite nursery.

Grasping Libby's hands, Matilda's voice trembled. "Libby, I know I keep saying it, but you truly are a blessing in our lives."

Libby folded Matilda into a warm embrace and said, "And I keep saying it back to you. It works both ways, my dear friend."

Rosie proudly presented little tinfoil packages, decorated with stickers, to Chance and Max and Mimi. "I wrapped them myself," she said, as she opened each one to give them the treat inside.

There were Christmas crackers to pull which caused Chance to bark and the cats to flee. Rosie asked to read aloud the jokes inside which Matilda and Libby then had to explain to her. They all wore the multi-colored paper crowns and answered questions from a deck of conversation starter cards that Libby had.

The questions were fun and the entire dinner time was filled with lively chat and laughter.

After the dinner had been savored by the three of them, Matilda insisted that she and Rosie help clean up despite Libby's protests. Later, they all expressed joy over the time they had spent together and sadness to see the day end. Rosie hugged Chance and Libby and the cats over and over when she said goodbye. Libby promised she and her family would call Rosie and Matilda on Christmas Day from Hawaii.

As Libby fell into bed that night she felt so fulfilled by the gift of their friendship and knew that the feelings were deeply reciprocated. She thought about the sayings that state that family is not always by blood, but often by choice.

How serendipitous it was that while she was separated from some and had lost an important part of her family, these new friends had come into her life and become family.

And all thanks to Chance. She chuckled softly at the play on words.

Chapter Twenty-Five

The secret Libby and Matthew were keeping from Jack and Kate was that Chance was going to go along with Libby to Hawaii. Libby did her research and booked with the airline that paid the most attention to the care of dogs they were transporting. She felt Chance would be well treated and she attached an air tag to his collar as further assurance she could keep track of his whereabouts.

The day before she left, Libby took over a small decorated Christmas tree for Don's room. She and Dorothy had put up garlands earlier in December, making the room as festive as possible even though they knew Don would not notice. It made Libby feel better to know she was making the effort.

She left glass containers with his favorite holiday treats and hoped he would find some enjoyment from them even as his appetite was diminishing.

After he picked at a dinner plate Libby brought from home, they went to the party room for a concert of Christmas carols with a local church choir. Later, as she tenderly kissed Don goodnight, Libby wished he could know how deeply she loved and missed him in her life. She left Chance cuddling on his lap until Don fell asleep and then, filled with a sadness she knew would always be part of her, Libby went home.

Somehow Chance seemed to feel this and stayed quietly close to her for the remainder of the evening. Slowly, after looking at photos, Libby filled her sadness with good memories of her life with Don. She knew those were the important thoughts to keep alive and she climbed into bed that night feeling grateful.

Their luggage was by the front door waiting for the early morning pick up by Patty for the drive to Tampa Airport.

Matthew and his family were waiting for Libby at the arrivals area at the Daniel K. Inouye International Airport in Honolulu. When Libby walked out with Chance leading the way, Jack and Kate could barely control their surprise and excitement.

Hawaiian music was playing and the greeters at the arrivals gate even placed a colorful lei around Chance's neck. Strangers smiled and exclaimed as he walked proudly by. Jack and Kate threw their arms around him and he responded with slurpy kisses and his tail wagging so fast his feet barely touched the floor.

He had grown into a fine-looking mature Lab, but the puppy part of his personality still showed up with his never-ending enthusiasm for everything.

"Grandma, this is the best surprise ever!"

A New Leash on Life

"How did we not know?"

"Chance is so handsome! So sweet!"

Libby knew this was going to be a Christmas to remember in an extra-special way.

Matthew had rented a spacious bungalow on a property bordering a beach with a large fenced in yard. A lush garden surrounded the house and Libby couldn't stop breathing in the sweet fragrances that wafted into the open living areas. The constant, rhythmic sound of the waves told her this would be the lullaby sending her to sleep in no time each night.

"This is perfect, Matt and Amy! It's even better than the website showed."

"It's spectacular," he agreed. "And we have a crate for Chance, toys and a comfy bed in your space in the guest wing in case he gets tired of being smothered with all of the attention."

"No worries about that," Libby replied. "He's going to be in doggy utopia for two weeks."

Matthew had researched dog-friendly hiking trails and beaches near them and on two very early mornings they followed trails before the day heated up. One particular trail brought them through a lush rainforest to a spectacular waterfall and another to a viewpoint that had a panoramic view over Pearl Harbour.

"There's such drama in the landscape here," Libby said to Amy and Matthew.

They both nodded in agreement. "I've never taken as many photos as I am on this trip," Amy said. "Everywhere we go is a visual feast!"

They talked about Matthew's job in Sydney. "Do you think your position in the company there may become permanent?" she asked.

Without hesitation, Matthew said, "There is a good chance of that, Mom, but it is not definite yet."

"Well, as much as I will miss having you close, I hope it happens for you. As I age, I am reminded of how important it is to take chances and experience new adventures while you are young."

"We worry about leaving you so far away," Matthew said.

Libby reached out to hug him and Amy. "There is nothing to worry about. The world has changed. We see each other all the time in our video calls and if you need to come home, a flight is not a problem. I am fine. In fact, I will be finer knowing you are having these wonderful opportunities. I live vicariously through them."

"Mom, you are the best. It's a tremendous relief to all of us to know you are fine and living your best life. We're thankful for your amazing friends, your good health, the care Dad is receiving ... and now, for Chance!"

Hearing his name, Chance bounded back to Libby from where he had been with Kate. They all laughed as he rubbed his head on her leg. "There's no question, Chance has made a major difference in my life."

Without fail, every day except one there was rain followed by the most magnificent, almost magical, rainbows. The showers were sometimes heavy tropical torrents and other times light sprinkles, but everything dried quickly.

Raindrops sparkled on the lush foliage which appeared brighter and the flowers more vibrant against the vivid blue sky.

A New Leash on Life

The family spent a lot of time at the beach. The long stretches of powdery golden sand invited barefoot walks followed by lazy naps under coconut palms.

The stunning blue and turquoise water was so clear that fish and coral could be seen in the protected bays without a snorkel. At other beaches, chunky black lava rock tumbled from the shore in dramatic contrast.

Chance loved the salt water and waves of the Pacific in Hawaii as much as he did the pool and calm Florida gulf at home. Everyone shrieked with laughter as they frolicked in the water with him and gasped at his sunset zoomies on the beach.

Jack and Kate begged to have him stay forever.

"Not happening!" Libby said. "He is too much a part of my life. Those zoomies are the same ones he does on our evening beach walks at home. I couldn't imagine my day ending without them."

Matthew and his family fell in love with Chance as Libby had. They told her they planned to put in a request for a pup from Leslie as soon as they knew a definite return date to Dragonfly Cove.

"And if it turns out we are staying here in Australia, we will most definitely get a pup as soon as possible. The kids insist it has to be a Labrador retriever. Go figure! Having Chance here has convinced us!"

"I love seeing how the two of you have bonded," Matthew said to his mother.

"Yes, thanks to you he has been the most wonderful unintended gift. I don't know what I would do without him now."

On Christmas Day, they had a video chat with a very excited Rosie and Matilda.

Rosie could not stop saying thank you again for all of

her gifts but also added several times, "Mrs. M, you and Chance need to get back soon because I miss you too much!"

"I can see there's also been some bonding going on there too, Mom," Matt teased Libby.

"Yes indeed. Another surprise Chance brought into my life."

Chapter Twenty-Six

On the return flight to Florida from Hawaii, Libby could not stop smiling. The days spent with her family had been filled with beauty and laughter as they made wonderful memories to treasure. There were few photos that did not include Chance.

A week after she had settled back in to her Florida routine, it was time for Libby, Deborah, Anne and Patty to gather at Marge's for their annual January party: the Belated Bubbly New Year's Noshfest.

For decades they had celebrated New Year's Eve together with their spouses. But as the years passed, other plans with family, travel, divorce and poor health interfered. Ten years ago, they decided that the third Saturday in January would be the forever designated women-only alternative. Dogs included, of course.

Champagne was on ice and each woman contributed one appetizer. Each year there was always a returning favourite along with new irresistible recipes.

Marge prepared a charcuterie board they swore could

win awards. It featured a selection of artisan cheeses, prosciutto, salami, chorizo, pâté, olives, grapes, figs, apples as well as almonds, walnuts, and candied pecans. Small pots of honey, mustards and fig jam, were set beside it along with a basket of freshly sliced baguettes.

The arrival was always chaotic as Einstein insisted on barking at all the dogs and they barked back. After a gentle reprimand to the parrot from Marge, he then squawked repeatedly "No barking! No barking!" until the dogs settled down.

Laughter set the tone for the evening.

The gathering progressed with the enjoyment of the food and sharing of recipes. The sound of the cork popping and bubbly champagne being poured into the flutes always elicited cheers. Its effervescence unfailingly created a lively ambiance.

They raised the delicate glasses and toasted. "To friendship, fun and another good year!"

There were many other toasts throughout the evening. The women looked back on all that had happened in the previous twelve months and wished each other the best they could hope for in the new year.

Dessert was unchanged by unanimous agreement through the years: Libby's shortbread and her mincemeat tarts.

The dogs and Einstein enjoyed their own treats. Later, a midnight walk with the dogs was a traditional part of the celebration. Marge had to tell Einstein they were all going to bed. She covered his cage so he would not feel left out as they silently tiptoed to the door.

"That parrot knows how to party!" was repeated every year. His vocabulary continued to increase and each year he added more woohoos, cheers and other assorted celebratory gleeful comments.

"I can never decide whether this celebration of ours is for the end of last year or the beginning of this one," Patty said. "But whatever it is, I cherish it."

Anne chimed in. "Our friendships are the gifts that keep giving. We have so many great memories to treasure."

There followed reminiscences of trips they had taken through the years and special occasions they had celebrated. Laughter filled the air and they shushed each other as it sometimes got out of control, tears pouring down cheeks. The kind of laughter only good friendships could cause.

Slipping back in to the house quietly, they changed into sleepwear, put out the dog beds and settled in for an all-nighter. After a few last bursts of laughter, some serious wishes and emotional hugs, sleep came quickly.

As January was coming to an end, Leslie sent birthday wishes reminding Libby that Chance would turn one at the end of February.

Libby called Leo to see if she had heard anything about a party, but nothing seemed to be planned.

Matthew accepted a long-term contract with his company to remain in Australia for at least five years.

At first Libby felt sad but then remembered her words to Matthew about taking chances and having adventures while they were young. She knew she would visit them at least once a year and their video chats would continue. She had lost the proximity of her family, but at the same time had gained a new one.

As their friendship deepened, Matilda confided to Libby more details of the troubled start to Rosie's young life. Libby felt strongly that they had come into each other's lives for a reason.

"From the time she was born she was surrounded by a lot of violence and rough talk. Her father was abusive to her mother in every way and eventually was killed in a fight." A horrified expression came onto her face and she stopped talking, her head shaking.

Libby took her hand and squeezed it gently as Matilda continued.

"Right in front of Rosie! She did not speak for a few years and then only when necessary. Truly, that did not change until Chance was with her day and night for that week."

Libby shook her head, shocked to consider the trauma Rosie had endured. Yet, deep inside this kind, bright little girl, innocence and strength had combined to build the will to survive, to look for the good and believe in love. Now she had found it.

"You and Chance have been true gifts in our lives. What a stroke of luck to have found you." Matilda said.

Libby felt choked with emotion before she replied, "I hope by now you realize you can trust me and I will always do everything I can to nurture Rosie in every way. I am grateful every day for the new family we have created together and the love we share."

🐾 🐾
🐾 🐾

Libby had been considering something for a while and after

A New Leash on Life

the intimate chats and disclosures Matilda had shared with her, she felt this was a good time to act.

With Matilda's permission, Libby and Rosie visited the local humane shelter. Rosie's birthday was coming soon and her gift from Libby and Matilda was for her to choose a kitten or adult cat to take home and love. They would shop later for the inevitable necessities.

Rosie was beside herself with joy at first. But after having a few days to absorb the news, she had become quite thoughtful about the situation.

"I know this will mean cat hair everywhere, but I like to vacuum and will make sure I take care of that. I will change the litter too and look after the meals."

Libby and Matilda smiled as she made these promises because they knew she would keep them. Rosie was like that.

On the special "gotcha day" as Rosie was calling it, Libby felt goosebumps as Rosie clutched her hand tightly when they entered the shelter. Her excitement was palpable. Rosie's gaze darted from one cat to another and she took her time carefully thinking through her choice.

Ultimately, she chose a tiny ginger colored, short-haired kitten with the brightest blue eyes. It had softly meowed and rubbed on her fingers when Rosie reached into the pen where it was playing with other kittens. It was a female they were told, just eight weeks old.

In a voice filled with joy, Rosie said, "I'm going to call her Goldie! Just like I called Chance before I knew his name when I thought he was a girl! Oh, I love her already ... but not quite as much as Chance. I will never love anyone more than Chance."

"We will see about that," Libby told her. "And it's okay if you do. She is yours to love as much as you want."

As they drove home, with Goldie snuggled in Rosie's lap, she said, "But I hope they will be best friends. Can I bring her over to meet Chance and Max and Mimi? She will be part of our family too."

"That will be great fun!" Libby said.

Chapter Twenty-Seven

The days began to grow longer with spring around the corner. At Serenity Palms, Doctor Sherin approached Libby about the possibility of having Chance go through training to become an official therapy dog.

"We have all observed here that Chance has the perfect personality for the work involved. A therapy dog brings comfort and affection to people around him and helps to relieve stress. We have all watched Chance visiting here for these many months. It's become obvious that he is a natural. Are you interested in training with him?"

Libby could hardly contain her excitement. "I would love to do that. What is involved?"

"Therapy dogs need certification from a reputable national organization. You would register and take a course with Chance. Certification is the final hurdle of the process which includes a temperament assessment, training, and you need to show you are in complete control of him. I daresay that's not a problem, from all I have seen."

Giving Chance a scratch on his back, the doctor said,

"Seriously, you seem to have the perfect combination. I do believe you were meant for each other."

Libby blushed, feeling a rush of pride from head to toe.

"For someone who never wanted to have a dog, I've certainly surprised myself," she said. "But really it is Chance who has made me this way. I can see how happy he is when people respond to him. It's as if he knows he's doing a good thing."

Doctor Sherin handed her a brochure. "Here is some information to get you started. I know the first step is to contact the American Kennel Club and register for the CGC program ~ the Canine Good Citizen. It's a 10-skill test that teaches good manners to the dog and responsible ownership to you. You will ace it immediately!"

That evening, as they snuggled on the couch, Libby lovingly stroked Chance's silky ears and gazed into his dark eyes that promised such unconditional love. She swallowed a lump in her throat as she felt her eyes well up. She knew she promised Chance unconditional love right back. Her heart filled as it did each day. How could she ever have imagined the joy and changes this dog had brought into her life.

In less than one year, Libby's family circle had grown. She, Rosie and Matilda had created a bond built on love, trust and the experiences they were making happen. Their shared values, interests, and beliefs brought them together as a family, eagerly embraced as well by Matthew and his family so far away.

What pleased Libby deeply about the therapy dog suggestion was the feeling that in this way she was connecting more to Don's life and to other residents at Serenity Palms. This was something she and Chance could contribute together. It was one more gift she was being given that would never have happened except for one thing.

All because of a dog.

Epilogue

Leslie's Story

Libby could hardly contain her excitement. What a love story Leslie had shared with her friends in Dragonfly Cove. Now they were honored and thrilled to see Leslie marry the stranger who unexpectedly came into her life and delivered a love of which she had only dreamed.

This was going to be such a special afternoon and, bonus, Libby had found the perfect dress. This was something that did not happen often to her. It was an off the shoulder, mid-calf style in a soft pink chiffon that was light as a feather and made her feel almost radiant. Chance sported a bowtie of the same fabric.

Rosie was thrilled to pieces to attend with her. "I feel like a princess in my new dress, Granny M." Matilda had insisted that Rosie be allowed to bestow the Granny title on Libby as well as time went on. Libby had been filled with pride and love to accept it.

Rosie had peppered her with questions about marriage and the wedding ceremony ever since she knew she was going to this one. Her excitement was high at being part of this expression of love and Libby overheard her having the sweetest chats with Chance about it.

They slipped into a row next to Leo. Loyal and True were lying quietly on the floor next to her. Their tails wagged as they stood up when they saw Chance. With a slight motion of Leo's hand, they lay down again after bumping noses with each other.

Leo had trained them well, Libby had noted during her frequent visits with them. As Chance had offered Libby a new opportunity to be happy, so had Leo's pups brought much the same to her. Leo had honored Vrai's memory by keeping the two dogs together and Libby watched as the love they all shared helped her friend slowly find her way through the mire of grief.

Libby asked Chance to lay down at her feet and he did so after gently bussing Leo.

Leo gave Rosie a big wink and a thumbs up as she looked at her dress.

The back yard filled quickly as friends waved and smiled to each other. And dogs ... there were so many dogs that Leslie had brought into the world in Dragonfly Cove.

Magical music began and Leslie walked down the aisle to the lovely rendition of *O Sole Mio* that a friend of Nico's played on his violin. The song title translated to 'Oh My Sun' and was perfect for them, as well as a traditional song played for the bride's walk at Italian weddings.

Leslie stood at the altar, staring into the gorgeous brown eyes of the man of her dreams—the man most people thought for a while didn't exist or was pretending to be someone he was not.

They would be having another ceremony in Italy, in a church surrounded by the friends and family of Nico's who couldn't travel, but Leslie had still insisted that they include a few familiar traditions into this day. He had even serenaded her the night before, making her blush and try to keep from giggling as he did his best to impress her.

After all this time of going back and forth to Italy, spending time in his home and then hers, getting to know the people who are important in each other's lives, it had all come down to this. A cozy backyard wedding behind the Sunny Cove Inn, surrounded by friends and family, and dogs. Always dogs but most of these were even more special. They were dogs who Leslie had worked to bring into the world and to deliver to people who needed them the most. Every dog had a destiny—always a life plan to be a comfort to someone, to help them through difficult times and to be their best friend.

Ethan cleared his throat and began. "Welcome, loved ones ... people and dogs. We are gathered here today to join Leslie and Nico in holy matrimony."

Ethan was a man transformed in the last year. Libby was happy to see he looked settled and no longer carried the burden he'd once dragged everywhere. He was their good friend now and had not only loaned the spectacular garden of his inn for the wedding, but he'd agreed to get certified to officiate the service. Melody was taking their wedding photos, and she was quite the professional, moving in and around like a ghost, barely seen as she got shots from every angle. Of course, Melody was also the reason for Ethan's transformation into a happy man.

Leslie carried a bundle of sunflowers, a reminder of the day she'd never forget.

It had started with a romantic beach picnic to watch the sunset, but that was nothing unusual for Nico to do. They often made it a point to be on the beach when the sun was setting, their favorite time of the day.

A New Leash on Life

This time he'd set sunflowers all around the blanket. Champagne chilled in a bucket with two crystal glasses nearby. A gorgeous vintage diamond ring suddenly was held before her, and hope glistened in Nico's eyes.

She had shared the story with everyone.

A dog barked and Leslie turned to see who it was.

It was Lily, Allison's dog, and she looked at them expectantly, as if to say, "Get on with it." Both were her flower girls and had done a beautiful job.

Allison had flourished in the time since getting Lily. Their story was one made for a movie—her dad finding out that the birth mother he never knew was right here in Dragonfly Cove. Allison, once insecure from being bullied, was doing so much better with a new dog and a sudden grandmother in her life.

Ethan continued. "This day is an acknowledgement of the next chapter in their lives together and everyone here will bear witness as Nico and Leslie affirm this bond formally and publicly. Nico, Leslie, please join hands."

Libby noticed Leslie's hands shake as she handed off her bouquet to Emily.

Then she took the hands that Nico held out.

"*Amore Mio*, I got you," he said softly. He smiled and the deep crinkles that she adored so much appeared around his eyes.

Suddenly, as Nico's warmth covered her hands and flowed up through her body, she was fine. No more trembling. He brought her so much peace. Her butterflies settled and all she saw was him, and their future.

"Nico and Leslie are here to mark this day not only by celebrating the love between themselves, but by also observing the love between all of us—including the love of their parents, siblings, extended family, best friends, and as many of Leslie's Labs that could come."

Another wave of chuckles went through the garden. Libby smiled as Rosie reached down and patted Chance's head.

"Without that love, today would be far less joyous," Ethan said.

Love. Such a short and simple word that held so much meaning. Libby gazed at Leslie and thought about how much her friend's life had transformed.

Leslie had told her she no longer felt lonely or abandoned. She had a circle of love around her, and so many stories of how her dogs had brought about more of it in their own lives.

And she had Nico.

She had told Libby he was the kindest and gentlest man she'd ever known. She had never been treated as the center of someone's world but that was exactly how she felt with him. Not only were they in love, but they were best friends, never wanting to be apart.

Nico looked especially handsome today in his fitted suit. He'd let the gray grow out more at his temple after she'd convinced him that she preferred his natural look, and in America, he was considered a Silver Fox. He'd laughed heartily at the conversation but took it to heart, embracing the path to growing older together gracefully.

They'd decided to split their time between Leslie's home in Dragonfly Cove and his in Italy, six months at a time, therefore she wouldn't be bringing as many dogs into the world as she'd had before. That was okay, too. Turns out that Nico was more financially secure than she'd thought. He wasn't rich, and neither was she, but they'd be comfortable as long as they were careful.

A New Leash on Life

The next words from Ethan were a blur, but when he said her name, she came back to the present. "Do you Leslie, take Nico to be your lawfully wedded husband?" Ethan asked. "To have and to hold, in sickness and in health, in good times and not so good times, for richer or poorer, keeping yourself unto him for as long as you both shall live?"

Libby saw Leslie swallow deeply, closing her eyes, before she nodded. "I do."

She noticed many friends reaching for tissues as Nico smiled.

"And do you, Nico, take Leslie to be your lawfully wedded wife? To have and to hold, in sickness and in health, in good times and not so good times, for richer or poorer, keeping yourself unto her for as long as you both shall live?"

"I do," he said, loudly and firmly.

Leslie and the guests laughed at his enthusiasm. Libby and Leo exchanged grins.

Libby was reminded how Leslie confided in her one day when she was back for a quick visit. They met for a coffee on the porch of the Beachside Brew Coffee shop and Leslie said she totally believed Nico would be there for her. Libby had felt such happiness for her.

Leslie had gone on to say she'd learned in the last year that Nico was a man of his word. She'd met his best friend's widow, Colette, in Italy and they had become close friends. Colette was Leslie's biggest window into Nico and what kind of person he was.

Colette had told Leslie of the last year of her husband's life as he was wasting away from the cancer in his body, and how Nico had come every single day, sitting with his best friend for hours, talking and caring for him. How he'd taken over all her husband's duties around the home, keeping her and the kids comfortable and never needing for anything.

How he'd gone off when the money ran out and paid their bills without her even asking. She said Nico was not only like a brother to her, but he'd been their angel during her darkest times, fulfilling the promise he'd made to her husband the day he'd gotten the prognosis that nothing more could be done.

"Now we come to the rings," Ethan said.

Kuno handed Nico his ring, and Emily gave Leslie hers.

Rosie stood on her tiptoes, eager to see everything that was going on.

Ethan continued. "A ring is an unbroken circle, with ends that have been joined together, and it represents your union. It is a symbol of infinity, and of your infinite love. When you look at these rings on your hands, be reminded of this moment, your commitment, and the love you now feel for each other. Nico, please place the ring on Leslie's finger and repeat after me."

Slowly and sensually, Nico slid the ring onto her finger, causing a chill to run through Leslie, a sneak peek of the long night to come.

Ethan spoke the words and Nico followed suit.

"Leslie, I give you this ring as a symbol of my love with the pledge: to love you today, tomorrow, always, and forever."

"And now, Leslie, place the ring on Nico's finger and repeat after me. Nico, I give you this ring as a symbol of my love with the pledge: to love you today, tomorrow, always, and forever."

Leslie slid the ring on Nico's finger and spoke the words, meaning every single one from the depths of her soul.

A New Leash on Life

Forever.

With the rings now on their fingers, Ethan spoke even louder. "Before these witnesses, you have pledged to be joined in marriage. You have now sealed this pledge with your wedding rings. By the authority vested in me by the great State of Florida, I now pronounce you man and wife! Nico, you may kiss your bride."

They'd talked about this part, and because Leslie was a bit shy, Nico had agreed to give her a chaste kiss on the lips, with more to follow later.

But he must've forgotten because before Leslie could even take a breath, Nico had her in his arms and was kissing her with a fervor only known in romance novels.

Rosie gave Libby a little nudge and put her hand over her mouth as she giggled.

Libby couldn't help but grin at her.

The funny thing was, Leslie told Libby days later—it felt so euphoric and genuine, her head spun with the emotion and sparks they created, oblivious to the hoots and whistles coming from all their loved ones gathered around them.

Finally, in the ruckus, a few of the dogs piped in and Libby heard Dorothy Starr call out grumpily for them to button it up so they could get to the reception, and everyone laughed.

This was it—Libby knew it was a feeling that Leslie had never known before. It was simple. She was right smack in the middle of the happily ever after she'd always dreamed of, and she was going to grab it and hang on for dear life. Libby had been there once too.

With all the romance in the air, Libby had been reminded of her own emotional wedding. The vows she and Don exchanged and the enchantment of the day. She was happy that she could call back those memories today. She could smile and feel good about them.

Libby accepted she had come a long way emotionally in the last year. Her blissful memories of the years with Don, including the challenges everyone experiences, would always be a part of her. Together they had shared such love and made memories. They had raised their son and embraced his family as it grew. There was much to celebrate. There were times in the last three years where she wondered if she would ever feel anything but sadness about all that as Don's life changed.

But she had rewired.

Now she knew she would forever treasure the love and joy of those years. She also knew there was much to anticipate going forward with Rosie and Matilda. She had another trip planned to Matthew and his family in Australia and the weekly video chats kept them all close, including Chance.

She looked down at him lovingly as he stood and stretched. Then Rosie whispered it was time to go. Libby chuckled as she added, "I saw cupcakes. Lots of cupcakes."

People were standing and moving to the reception area, while Libby was caught up in her thoughts. So many people had said to her during the last few years, and she now knew it to be absolutely true, life goes on.

And, in her case she was reminded each day, all thanks to a dog.

The End

A New Leash on Life

*Don't miss a Dragonfly Cove book! *

(All the books are stand alones and can be read in any order.)

Book 1: Pick of the Litter
   Book 2: Collar Me Crazy by Kay Bratt
   Book 3: Hearts Unleashed by Tammy L. Grace
   Book 4: Back in the Pack by Barbara Hinske
   Book 5: Loyal & True by Ev Bishop
   Book 6: Coming Home to Heel by Jodi Allen Brice
   Book 7: Unleashed Melody by Julie Carobini
   Book 8: Teacher's Pet by David Johnson
   Book 9: A New Leash on Life by Patricia Sands

Acknowledgments

I hope you enjoyed reading this story as much as I enjoyed writing it. As a lifelong owner of dogs, cats and even a pet squirrel, the sentiments in the story come straight from my heart.

As you may know from my series of books set in the south of France, I coincidentally have a yellow Labrador retriever named Picasso who is a big star in all seven books. As the series progressed, more pets were added to join him ... even some donkeys and chickens. So, as you can see, I do have a deep love of animals and writing about the joy of owning a dog is something that brings me great pleasure. All of the books in this series have been such fun to read.

As always, there are so many people to thank for getting this book to publication: Kelly Siskind, for her excellent editing skills and copy editor, Dione Benson, as well as cover designer Elizabeth Mackey. I would get nothing done without the help of Kerry Schafer (Author Genie) who, among other things, did the formatting to turn my manuscript into a REAL book.

I am eternally grateful to my wonderful advance readers for the time they take to read, review and comment about my books. In particular, Gail Johnston, a voracious reader of all genres, who reads everything I write from the beginning of some dreadful first drafts and can spot a typo a mile away. We've been close friends for over fifty years and

I value her insight and honesty. She helps keep me sane and laughing even through the difficult days.

Bookstagrammers who read and talk about our books are so important to authors. It would be impossible to name all of them here, but it goes without saying that the tremendous effort they put into reading and reviewing books of all genres is valued and respected by every author I know.

A big bouquet of thanks also goes to each author in this series for the fabulous sense of community that has existed through the past year as we each wrote our stories and worked together on how to bring this entertaining reading experience to booklovers everywhere. Special kudos to the awesome Kay Bratt, Tammy L. Grace, and Ev Higginson our fearless leaders in developing the series.

Thank you for reading A New Leash on Life and for telling your friends about the series. Thanks also for leaving short reviews on Amazon, Bookbub and Goodreads, which are so helpful to authors. I would love to have you sign up for my monthly newsletter (lots of giveaways, writing news and always photos about my travels in France).

I hope your hearts are filled by all of the stories in this series and that you will feel excited to explore the many great novels you see listed by each author.

Happy reading!

About the Author

Patricia Sands lives two hours north of Toronto, but her heart's other home is the South of France. An avid traveler, she spends part of each year on the Cote d'Azur. Her award-winning 2010 debut novel, *The Bridge Club,* is a book club favorite. *The Promise of Provence,* which launched her three-part Love in Provence series was a finalist for a 2013 USA Best Book Award and a 2014 National Indie Excellence Award, an Amazon Hot New Release in April 2013, and a 2015 nominee for a #RBRT Golden Rose award in the category of romance.

Drawing Lessons, Sands' fifth novel, also set in the south of France, was released by Lake Union Publishing in 2017 and was a Finalist in the Somerset Literary Book Award 2019. *The Villa des Violettes* miniseries released in 2019/20 and Book 4 was published in December 2023. This series carries on with the characters from the Love in Provence trilogy.

Her most recent novel, *The Secrets We Hide*, published August, 2022 and received the 2023 Book Excellence Award for Women's Fiction, the 2024 International Impact Book Award for Women's Literary Fiction, and a Finalist in Women's Fiction in the 2024 American Fiction Book Awards.

In March, 2023, *Lost At Sea*, Book 8 in the nine-book

Sail Away series was published. In December, 2024, *A New Leash on Life*, Book 9 in the Dragonfly Cove Dog Park series will be published.

A lifelong photographer, follow Patricia on Instagram @psands.stories .

Find out more at Patricia's Facebook Page, Amazon Author Page or her website where there are links to her books, social media, and monthly newsletter that has special giveaways and sneak peeks. She would love to hear from you!

Made in the USA
Las Vegas, NV
11 March 2025